Dancing Through the Storm

A Step In Time Book one

Second edition

Stacey Broadbent

When all else fails...
Dance!

Contents

Chapter 1

Sacha swung her leg over Dane, straddling him as he lay on the bed with his arms behind his head. She licked her ruby red lips seductively, as she ran her hands up and down his strong, muscular chest. There was a mischievous glint in her eye. Dane laughed, circling his hands around her waist.

"What?" she asked innocently.

"You're up to something. I can see it in your eyes." He grinned. "What do you want?"

"Who? Me?" She pointed one perfectly manicured nail at her own chest, eyes wide and virtuous. Dane pulled her towards him, lifting his head to meet hers before planting a kiss on her lips.

"Yes, you, little Miss Innocent." He kissed her again, wrapping his arms tighter around her waist. She unfolded her legs so that she was now lying on his chest, her legs intertwined with his. The kiss deepened, and Sacha let out a low moan as she ran her fingers through his hair. Dane's hands made a slow track down her back, his fingers easing under the waistband of her jeans. His arousal was obvious as she moved her hips against his, teasing him. She smiled against his lips.

"I think I might go," she whispered, pushing herself up off the bed. It was one of her favourite things to do to him; get him all riled up and then pretend she was leaving. She liked to be in control and have him beg her.

"You've got to be kidding me!" he whined as he sat up on his elbows, looking at her with hooded eyes. "Come on, it was just getting good, baby," he crooned, reaching for her.

"Mmm? It was, wasn't it?" She arched her back, stretching her arms above her head. Her already short top lifted, exposing her midriff. As expected, Dane lurched off the bed and sank to his knees in front of her, planting soft kisses on her bare stomach. His hand reaching around to cradle her behind as he did so.

"You… are… so… sexy." He kissed his way up her body as his hands slowly slipped her top over her head. With his chest pressed against hers, he whispered, "Please don't go."

"Well… seeing as you asked so nicely," she purred in his ear, her tongue darting out; something she knew drove him crazy. He cupped her behind in his hands and lifted her into his arms, his mouth crushing hers as he carried her towards the bed. "I guess I can stay a little longer," she murmured.

"What time did you wanna head down to the studio?" Sacha asked as she sauntered back in from the shower, wearing only a towel. Ensuring the knot was secured, she bent down to sift through a pile of clothes on the floor. Dane had given her a drawer to use when she moved in, but she preferred a bit of chaos.

"You know, you're really gonna have to stop wiggling your arse at me if you want to get to the studio." Dane watched with a grin as she deliberately bent down even lower.

"I don't know what you're talking about it." She winked before selecting a tight red tee with a low-cut neckline, some jeans and red heels to match. With a look over her shoulder, she lifted her arm and dropped the towel, walking away from him with a smirk. She giggled at his sharp intake of breath.

"You're really not helping the situation by parading around like that," he groaned, flopping onto his back.

Sacha shimmied into her jeans, peeking back over her shoulder. "Come on, get ready!" She pulled her top over her head and fluffed her hair as she turned to face him. "I wanna get my groove on!" She wiggled her hips provocatively.

"Alright, alright." Dane pushed himself up off the bed and loped over to his drawers, pulling out a black shirt and some jeans. It was Thursday; dance night. Without fail, every week, they would drop everything to go to their studio, Latin Flava, and then on to Feeney's Bar afterwards for a night of social dancing.

They had both started dancing salsa a year ago and had had an instant attraction to each other. Sacha had a sexy, sassy way of moving; and Dane couldn't help but watch her every move. With her curvy figure and fiery attitude, it was clear to see she was born to salsa. There was a natural chemistry between them when they danced, and it hadn't taken long before they were more than just partners, both on and off the dancefloor.

If Dane was honest, he had started dancing to pick up chicks, and lucky for him, he happened to be good at it. Sacha was a firm believer that you could tell how a man was in the bedroom by the way he moved his hips on the dancefloor, and Dane's hips didn't lie. She was drawn to him like the proverbial moth to a flame. He towered above her tiny five-foot frame, but her attitude more than made up for her small stature. They made quite the striking couple really; she with her jet-black hair and pale complexion, and he with his olive skin, hair the colour of chocolate and eyes to match. It was no wonder they were the 'it' couple.

Both as dedicated as the other, they breezed through classes, practising at home and out at Feeney's. They lived and breathed dance.

Their teacher, Rachel, had suggested they work towards entering the Nationals at the end of the year. Competitive by nature, they jumped at the chance to show off.

Dane had been working on a choreography he was sure would 'wow' the judges. He had been watching a lot of lessons online, learning lifts and dips that they could incorporate into their dance. Sacha was more than happy to let him do all the hard work; she just had to make it look good, which happened to be her forte.

As with any collaboration though, they had their fair share of heated discussions, and both being just as stubborn as the other, neither one was willing to back down.

Sacha enjoyed antagonising him. She found it thrilling to see the fire in his eyes when they fought—it made the make-up even better.

"Hey, did I tell you I invited my mate Jessie along tonight? He's going to meet us at Feeney's to have a look," Dane said while ruffling a hand through his hair to give it that messy look.

"Jessie? Have I met him?" she asked, knowing all too well that she had.

"He was at that party we went to a few weeks back."

"Hmm. I think I know who you mean. Is he looking to pick up?"

Dane laughed, "Yeah, he's been going through a dry spell. I told him dancing is a great way to meet chicks, so he thought he'd tag along." He came up behind her, wrapping his arms around her waist and planting a kiss on the back of her neck. "It worked for me, didn't it?" His lips brushed below her ear.

"Sure did, babe." She spun around in his arms, stretching up to caress the back of his neck before pulling him down to kiss her again. "You ready?"

"And willing," he replied, grabbing his leather jacket from the coat hook. "We should make it in time for the advanced class. A bit of a warmup before Feeney's."

"Perfect."

Down at the studio, Sacha strutted in as if she owned the place, dropping her bag in the corner and jumping to the front of the line for warmups. She motioned for Dane to join her up front.

"You know all these moves. Let someone else get up front," he whispered, taking her hand and attempting to drag her away.

"I'm just giving them another style to emulate." She winked. Dane smiled and shook his head. Being one of the better dancers had given her quite the ego—not that she didn't already possess a rather large one. She oozed confidence in everything she did. And Dane had a thing for women with confidence.

Looking around the studio, he could see that she actually had a point. Some of the other girls in class were watching her every move and trying their best to copy her. He couldn't blame them; she did have an amazing style all of her own. No matter what she did, somehow it always looked effortless and sensual. It was no wonder the other girls wanted to be like her. There was something so intoxicating about her—girls wanted to be her, and guys wanted to be with her. He saw the way they looked at her, undressing her with their eyes. He knew she loved the attention too, and sometimes she did get a touch flirty on the dancefloor, but it didn't really bother him, in fact, he liked knowing they all wanted her, so long as he was the one who got to go home with her every night.

The combo they were being shown this evening was simple but beautiful. Sacha added in her own personal styling, making it her own. After the lesson, when music was playing in the background, they had a friend film them dancing the new combo. Dane knew others were running for their phones to secretly film them too, but he just grinned and put on a show, like always. Dane was nothing if not a performer at heart.

They danced as if a spotlight was on them, and everyone faded into the background. It wasn't until the song ended that they came up for air and realised a circle had formed around them. Their classmates clapped and cheered, egging them on. Dane grinned, spinning Sacha out to take a bow, then he followed suit. Anything to keep an audience entertained.

At Feeney's, later that evening, Sacha and Dane joined their friends at a table near the dancefloor. While Sacha changed her shoes, Dane went to get them some drinks from the bar. He was still buzzing from their mini performance at the studio, and it only spurred him on to complete their competition routine. He couldn't wait to see how people reacted to what he'd come up with. If his classmates thought what they did tonight was good, they were going to be blown away at the comps.

Leaning against the bar, Dane gazed around the room, checking out who was already here. A few new faces, but mainly all regulars; typical of a Thursday evening.

He caught site of a familiar face walking through the door and, with a grin on his face, he raised his hand to wave and catch Jessie's attention.

"You made it!" Dane called, slapping his friend on the back as he led him back to the bar. "What are ya drinking?"

"Jack and coke." He reached for his wallet, but Dane waved it away.

"On me, man." He paid for their drinks and they made their way back to the table.

"Hey, everyone, this is Jessie. He's come to have a look at what we do." Dane made the rounds, introducing him to everyone. "You remember Sacha?" he asked as he moved to stand behind her.

"Yeah, of course. Nice to see you again." He nodded in her direction.

"You too. So, you're gonna be one of us then?" she asked, a glint in her eye.

"Ah, yeah maybe. I saw you and Dane dance at that party. It looked pretty hot." He grinned. "If I could get a hot chick like you to dance with me like that, I'd be in heaven," he joked.

"Well, you never know. Your wish just might come true," she purred, watching him take his jacket off.

"Here's hoping." He winked, pulling a seat out to sit down. His eyes seemed to soak in his surroundings as they followed a couple out onto the dancefloor.

"Hey, you wanna dance?" Dane offered his hand to Sacha. "We can show him a couple things?"

"Sure thing, baby." She took his hand and they made their way to the floor. The tempo switched from a fast-paced salsa to a sensual bachata—exactly the kind of dance Sacha shined in. Dane circled his arms around her waist, pulling her in close as they started to move their feet and hips in sync. She wrapped her arms behind his neck, leaning her head against his chest as they moved. Dane lowered his hands to her hips, slowly pulling her closer so that her body was rolling towards his with every step. He changed his grip ever so slightly, giving the signal for her to twist her body side to side with the beat. They continued this flawless, and somewhat erotic dance around the floor. Every step he took, she mirrored. Every move followed to perfection. Slowly bringing her hands up above her head, he trailed his fingers down her every curve until they landed on her hips again. With a flick of his wrist, she spun between his hands until her back rested against his chest, and they continued to sway like this until the last notes of the song rang out.

"Wow." Jessie stared, his mouth agape. "I couldn't take my eyes off you guys. That was... amazing! Damn sexy too! You're one lucky guy,

Dane." He slapped a hand on Dane's shoulder as he joined him at the table.

"Yeah, I know." He threw his arm around Sacha's shoulders.

"You wanna give it a go?" Sacha asked Jessie with a lopsided grin and a quirk of her brow.

"I don't know. I don't think my hips can move like that."

"Sure they can." She grinned, leaning into him. "Trust me." She took his hand and gently pulled him up out of his seat. "Just put your hands here." She placed his hands on her lower back. "And step in close so you can feel my hip movement." Jessie looked to Dane as if asking permission.

"Go for it, man! I trust you." Dane laughed.

Sacha put her hands on Jessie's shoulders and shuffled in close so that their thighs were touching, she nudged his knee out with hers, slipping her leg in between his.

"We stand this way so that we don't knock knees," she said, looking up at him as he laughed nervously. "Now, you're going to step sideways, starting with your left leg." She moved slowly, saying each movement aloud. "Step, together, step, hip." She flicked her hip up to one side then back down again. "And then we go back the other way. Right, together, right, hip." She pulled back, smiling. "See? You *can* do it. You just did the basic bachata step."

Jessie huffed out a breath. "Well, that wasn't nearly as scary as I thought it would be." He chuckled, bringing his hand up to rake it through his hair. "Can we try it again?"

"Sure. Go side-to-side a few times, get a feel for it." She counted the steps as they went, emphasising the hip movement, so he could feel the way to do it.

"The guy's a natural!" Dane slapped his friend on the back. "The great thing about bachata is that you don't even need to know lots of fancy steps. You can just go around the dancefloor doing those basic steps, feeling the music and it'll still look great." They took a seat back at the table, Dane grabbing Sacha and pulling her onto his lap. "Not to mention, you get to dance up close and personal with the ladies." He winked.

"You should come around sometime, we can show you some stuff," Sacha suggested.

"Yeah? I'd like that." Jessie grinned, swiping a hand across his brow. "Are you free this weekend?"

Chapter 2

Dane rolled over, his body searching for the warmth of Sacha's. Wrapping his arm around her middle, he pulled himself in closer, snuggling up against her back. His fingertips lightly brushed her stomach, tracing circles over her bare skin. His hands trailed down and around her hips, over her waist, and up to her shoulder, before making their way back down her arm, to her stomach once more. Her breath quickened as his hands slowly wandered over her body. She gently arched her back as he began nuzzling her neck—the part of her that was extremely sensitive. He kissed and licked a trail from her shoulder to her ear, making her wriggle.

"Good morning," he whispered as he continued his slow torment.

"Mmmm," she murmured, arching her back further, pushing her body into his with more intensity. Unable to contain himself any longer, he gripped her hip and rolled her towards him, lowering his lips to hers. She raked her hands through his hair and down his back, digging her nails in. Wrapping her legs around his waist, she pulled him on top of her.

"God, I love you," he said, looking into her eyes as he positioned himself over her.

"Back at ya, baby," she said with a grin as she lifted herself up to kiss him again.

"You're so damn beautiful."

"You're not so bad yourself." She leaned in to whisper in his ear. "Now stop talking."

Sacha sat on the side of the bed, blankets draped casually around her middle. She stretched her arms above her head, loosening her muscles before getting up. Glancing over her shoulder, she could see Dane peacefully snoring. Grabbing her silk robe from the back of the door, she slipped it over her shoulders and padded to the bathroom. She loved nothing more than a little morning action but lazing in bed afterwards was not really her thing. She splashed some cold water on her face to freshen up before changing into leggings and a singlet, ready for a run. Keeping her body curvy and toned didn't happen by itself. It required a rigorous exercise regime. Sure, dancing helped a lot too, but there was something to be said about being out in the fresh air.

Switching on her iPod, she peered into the bedroom to check if Dane was still sleeping. As suspected, he was out to it. *No stamina, that guy.* She grinned to herself as she grabbed her keys and headed out the door.

Running was like breathing to Sacha; it came naturally. She liked that she didn't really have to push herself to keep going, she just did. Always had, in fact. It made it easier for her to let her mind wander. She did some of her best thinking while pounding the pavement. Today was no different. Jessie was coming over tonight, and there was a lot they had to get done before then—neither of them were very domesticated, so a mad dash clean-up normally ensued when visitors were expected.

She made a mental list of chores: wash last night's dishes, wipe down benches, vacuum lounge, prepare a salad and get some sausages out of the freezer. She wasn't much of a cook; sausages, chips and salad—that was the extent of her culinary skills. Dane didn't seem to mind though. What she lacked in domestic skills, she more than made up for in other areas.

In her mind, men were simple creatures; keep them happy in the bedroom, have beer in the fridge and snack food readily available, and they were sorted. Of course, it helped to have a great rack too. Sacha was well aware of the stares she got from men. And women for that matter. In fact, she quite enjoyed it. If showing a bit of cleavage was going to get her what she wanted, then why not flaunt what she had? If there was one thing her dear old mama had taught her, it was that seduction is the key to everything.

"Baby, you can work hard every day to make piss-all money, like all them other mugs out there, or you can use what the good Lord gave you and get

everything your little heart desires," she'd say, while puffing on a cigarette and taking a swig of bourbon. *"See, honey, men? They're stupid. Don't think with their brains, they think with their dicks, and that's a fact. You, my girl, have been blessed with boobs and a booty that men will find irresistible. Show 'em a bit of skin, a good time in the bedroom, and you'll want for nothing, I can promise you that."*

She had been only too happy to share her 'tricks of the trade' with her, and Sacha had been eager to lap up her words of wisdom. It wasn't long before dear old mama was also benefitting from the exotic looks of her daughter; their weekends were spent parading around bars, looking for men to approach. Sacha would distract them with her 'charms' while Mama would empty their wallets. But when Mama started trying to pimp her out, she'd decided it was time to go out on her own.

She refined her skills to acquire more than just pocket change, without having to 'go all the way'. She was pretty good at it too. There were various degrees to her seduction techniques—depending on what she wanted out of it. A little flirting to get discount in a store, a show of cleavage to have her drinks bought for the night.

With this mastered, she hadn't really had to work a day in her life. Men would fall over themselves just to buy her a drink. As if *that* would make her go home with them. Please! They'd need to do a lot more than buy a drink to get into *her* pants. No, she just made them think they stood a chance, until she got what she wanted. Contrary to popular belief, she hadn't been around the block with every guy in town—only the ones she could benefit from.

Dane was no exception. She could see his potential instantly and knew they could go far in the dancing world—the fact that he was hot was an added bonus. He'd been lured in, like so many others before him—flash him a smile, laugh at his stupid jokes, and wiggle her arse in his direction—it had been all too easy. Now, he would do anything for her. Hell, she practically lived with him, rent free. He was just as big a schmuck as the rest of them.

To be fair, he did treat her like a queen, so she didn't really mind doing extra things for him. Not to mention, the sex was pretty good. Truth be told, she had grown quite fond of him. Originally her intentions had been for them to be together long enough for her to get to the top. Now, however, she was reconsidering this. He had made the fatal mistake of introducing her to Jessie.

Ah, Jessie. Now there was a beautiful specimen of a man. Tall and muscular—it was obvious he worked out—with piercing green eyes and sandy blond hair. She had definitely noticed him at that party they had been to, and now he was coming to their place— dangerous territory.

She could've forgotten about him, had he not shown up at Feeney's. Like Dane, he too had potential and she was good at bringing that out in men. There was no doubt in her mind that she could do the same for Jessie.

Dane was a brilliant dancer, but he held no challenge for her anymore and boredom was something that didn't sit well with Sacha. She needed the excitement. The thrill of the chase, so to speak. Dane had been a worthy opponent for a while at least. Plus, he had completely choreographed their routine, so she had barely had to lift a finger. But the spark had gone. She had just been going through the motions to get them to the comps, and then she had planned on ending it. Jessie was like the light at the end of the tunnel, and she *had* to have him.

Chapter 3

Sacha sauntered through the door, completely unaffected by her run. Not a hair out of place, or a drop of sweat to be seen. Sometimes Dane wondered if she was actually running at all. Not that he was one to talk. He had never been much of a fitness junky; he was lucky enough to have a fast metabolism, so found weight was never really a problem.

"Coffee?" he asked as she breezed past.

"Just gonna jump in the shower, but I'll have one when I get out, thanks."

Dane took another bite of his toast before flicking the switch on the jug and grabbing two mugs from the cupboard. He scooped coffee and sugar into both cups, then retrieved the milk from the fridge. As soon as he opened the lid, the stench of stale milk hit his nose.

"Ugh, that's nasty." He threw on some trainers, then knocked on the bathroom door. "We're out of milk! I'm just gonna shoot to the shop!"

"Okay!" Sacha yelled back.

"You need anything else?"

"Nah, I'm good, thanks!"

Shovelling the last of the toast in his mouth, he grabbed his keys from the bench and jogged out the door. The dairy was only a five-minute walk from their place, which was handy for times like these.

Armed with his bottle of green-top milk and a newspaper, Dane made his way to the counter. There was a leggy blonde standing in front of him, trying to choose between a Picnic bar and a Snickers.

"Just get both," he said with a grin.

"Huh?" She looked up.

"Oh, I said, just get both. You'll regret it if you don't."

"Hmm." She looked back at the bars before grabbing one of each, nodding to the cashier and handing over her cash. "Thanks," she said as she passed Dane.

Glancing back over his shoulder, he saw her eyes flick to his before she went out the door. She had given him the hint of a smile. He stepped up to the counter to pay for his things.

"Oh crap!" the cashier said. "She left her keys here."

"Hey, no problem, I'll go call her back." Dane jogged to the door. "Miss!" he called. "Excuse me!" He ran after her. She quickened her pace.

Really?

He reached out and tapped her on the shoulder. She spun around, her hands balled into fists.

"Whoa." He held his hands up. "I'm not going to hurt you. You just left your keys back at the shop." He pointed his thumb back.

"Oh. Well, that's a little embarrassing. I'm so sorry I freaked out. I just heard you running towards me and panicked." She giggled nervously.

"Hey, it's all good. It's good to be cautious." He smiled. "Come on, I'll walk you back."

"Thanks." She clasped her hands in front of her as she bounced towards the store. Dane couldn't help but notice how beautiful her smile was. In fact, he had to admit, she was quite stunning. Not that he would ever do anything to jeopardise what he had with Sacha. No other woman could compare. That didn't mean he couldn't admire another woman's beauty though.

"Found her," he announced when he walked back up to the counter.

"Thanks so much," she said to the cashier. "I'd forget my head if it wasn't screwed on." She laughed and turned to leave. "Thanks again. Maybe I'll see you around." She grinned, and then bounced out the door once more.

Sacha was out of the shower by the time he got home, and dancing around the lounge with music blaring. She was wearing the tiniest pair of denim shorts and a figure-hugging singlet. Definitely a sight to behold. He sure was a lucky guy.

"You took your time!" she yelled over the music, shimmying her way over. Dane loved it when she was playful like this.

"Had to help a damsel in distress," he said, wrapping his arms around her waist and pulling her gyrating body into his.

"Was she pretty?" She pouted.

"Not as pretty as you," he answered, kissing her softly.

"That's alright then. Am I still getting that coffee?"

"But of course." He went into the kitchen, adding the milk to their cups and re-boiling the jug.

"What time is Jessie coming over tonight?" she asked, kneeling on the couch in front of the breakfast bar so she could watch him.

"Around seven, I think. What are we drinking tonight?"

"Whatever you're buying." She grinned.

"Oh, it's like that, is it?"

"Yup."

"You might have to pay me back in other ways then." He winked.

"Whatever do you mean?" She blinked, an innocent expression on her face.

"I'm sure you can think of something," he teased.

"Hmm." She climbed off the couch, walking behind him. "You mean, like this?" She snaked her hands around his waist, unbuttoning his jeans.

"Mmmm, that could work," he said, closing his eyes as she began to stroke him.

"You like that?" she whispered.

"Mmhmm," he murmured.

"Well…" She removed her hand and slapped him on the arse. "You'll just have to wait till later." She grinned, grabbing her coffee off the bench, and stepping out of reach.

"Oh, really? Two can play at that." He lunged for her.

"Uh-uh! I've got a hot drink in my hand!" She squealed, holding her cup up for him to see.

"You'll just have to stay still then, won't you?" He ran his hand down her back, cupping her behind.

"We'll never get anything done at this rate!" She giggled.

"Cleaning is over-rated," he said, lowering his head to nibble her ear.

"Okay, okay! Let me put the coffee down first." He lifted his arm, giving her space to reach through to the bench before throwing her over his shoulder. She shrieked, giggling, as he carried her back to the bedroom.

Their morning was spent in various stages of undress, until Sacha finally dragged herself to the bathroom to shower once more. She didn't fancy being caught in the act when Jessie arrived. It would hardly help her cause.

Dane was busy washing dishes when she traipsed back to the bedroom, wrapped in her towel. She carefully selected the right outfit. Something that looked casual but at the same time, showed off her curves. A pair of faded jeans with rips down the front that moulded to her perfectly formed body, paired with her favourite vintage tee. She slicked her hair back into a ponytail, put a pair of hoop earrings in and slathered on some ruby red lipstick.

She could hear Dane starting up the vacuum cleaner in the lounge. She had trained him well. A little bit of horseplay and she barely had to lift a finger. She sashayed into the lounge.

"Thank you, baby." She winked as she walked through to the kitchen. The sausages were still thawing on the bench, so she put them in the fridge to finish off. Pulling open the veggie drawer, she grabbed a lettuce, capsicum, tomatoes and cucumber. She retrieved a chopping board from the cupboard, and slowly began slicing and dicing the veggies before adding them to a bowl.

"I'm going to head down to the liquor store before Jessie gets here. Any preference?"

"I always like bourbon, but whatever you want, baby," she cooed as she continued dressing the salad.

"Okay, won't be long." He gave her a quick kiss and grabbed his keys from the bench.

"I'll be here," she said. She wrapped cling film over the top of the bowl and put it back in the fridge. Looking around, she could see that Dane had pretty much done all the cleaning. With no plans of doing any more work, she switched her iPod on again, and made a playlist for the evening.

She was happily sitting on the couch with her feet up, flicking through a magazine when Dane came back, black bags in hand.

"You look busy." He grinned.

"Always." She put her magazine down. "What did you get me?"

"Bourbon, of course."

Sacha clapped her hands. "Ooh thank you, baby." She stood on tippy toes to kiss him. "I've got the salad and sausages in the fridge. I'll start cooking just before seven," she said, swiping the bag from his hand and pulling the bottles out. Twisting the cap off, she tipped it towards him. "You want one?"

"Sure, why not?"

"So, what stuff did you want to show Jessie tonight?" she asked as she stuck her head in the freezer to find the ice cubes.

"Maybe a little more bachata, a bit of salsa. We'll just see how he goes."

She topped the glasses off with cola. "Okay, good idea. He did seem quite keen on the bachata."

"Who wouldn't be, dancing with a hot thing like you?" He pulled her onto his lap, sloshing the drinks over her hands.

"Hey! You're making me spill the drinks!" She laughed, holding her hands up high and licking the liquid trickling down her wrist.

"You know? I really don't care." He grinned, finding the ticklish spot between her ribs. She squirmed away from his wandering hands, giggling and squealing as she did.

Chapter 4

"Mate, come in!" Dane held the door open for Jessie. "Welcome to our humble abode." He rolled his arm in the direction of the lounge.

"Thanks, man. I wasn't sure what you were drinking, so I brought beer and bourbon." Jessie held up his bag of goodies.

"It's gonna be a good night!" Dane laughed. "You hungry? Dinner's just about ready I think."

"Sweet. I'm starving." The boys walked through to the kitchen, putting Jessie's beer in the fridge and popping one open. "You want one?" he offered.

"Sure," Dane said, helping himself to one. "How 'bout you, babe?"

"Yeah, sure, why the hell not?" She grinned. "You boys want eggs with your sausages?"

"Oh, I don't mind. Whatever you guys want."

"Ooh, I could really go for some eggs actually, babe. Fried?"

"It's the only kind I make." She laughed. "You wanna get the plates out, while I cook 'em up?"

"But of course, m'lady." Dane stooped into a low bow before going to the cupboard. Jessie stood at the breakfast bar, watching with a smile on his face. "What?" Dane asked.

"It's good to see you happy, man. Sacha's good for you."

"She sure is." He planted a kiss on her cheek before setting the plates down on the bench.

"Oh crap."

"What's up?"

"I broke the egg yolk."

"Eh. It's all good. It's gonna get all mushed up inside anyway," Dane reassured, giving her a pat on the behind.

"Yeah, it's actually the way I like my eggs. Yolks are so over-rated," Jessie quipped while Sacha flipped the eggs over. She gave them a few seconds before scooping them onto the plates and dishing up the rest of the food.

"Whatever. You're just being nice." She looked up at Jessie with a smile. "Thanks."

"No really. It's just like my mum used to make." He took the plate from her hand. "Thanks for cooking."

"You're welcome. I don't do it often, so you better enjoy it while you can," she said before taking a large gulp of her beer. "Oh God. That's awful." She laughed, wiping her mouth with the back of her hand. "I don't know what you guys see in this shit. Gimme a bourbon any day." She offered the bottle to Dane.

"It's not for everyone I guess." He chuckled. "Here, I'll make you a drink. You sit and eat." He jumped up from his seat and poured her another bourbon and cola.

"Now that's a drink." She took a sip and sighed contentedly. "So, Jessie, what have you been up to today?"

"I spent the morning in the gym. Not much after that, I'm afraid."

"Ah, you're a gym nut. I thought you might be." She made a point of checking him out. "I like to run myself."

"Yeah? What about you, Dane? Does Sacha drag you out too?"

"Me?" he scoffed. "That'd be the day!" He patted his stomach. "This body of perfection you see before you is all thanks to good genes and dancing. I'm one of those people you love to hate." He laughed.

"Bastard!" Jessie and Sacha said together.

"Hey, it's not my fault I'm so damn hot." He held his arms out, strutting about the room like Mick Jagger.

"Poser."

"You love it."

Sacha rolled her eyes, laughing. "If you say so."

"So, are we gonna dance or what?"

"You up for it, Jessie?" she asked as she cleared the plates away and poured herself another drink.

"Sure, I'll give it a crack."

"What do you want to do? Salsa? Bachata?"

"I did really like that one we did the other night at Feeney's."

"Yeah, it's our favourite too, eh babe?" Dane said, grabbing her hand and pulling her in to a closed position. "This is your basic hold—it's the same for most dances. You want to have your hand on her shoulder blade, so you can lead her, like this." Dane gently but firmly, placed pressure on Sacha's back, signalling for her body to turn in each direction. "So, the basic step for bachata looks like this. Step left, together, left and hip. Then, right, together, right and hip." He demonstrated both by himself and with Sacha. "Now you try."

Sacha stepped in close, placing her hand on his shoulder.

"Ready?" she asked, looking up at him.

"Yup." He stared down at his feet as he began to move. "Left, together. Left and hip," he said under his breath. "Right, together. Right and hip."

"Good, now try doing it a little more fluidly. Not so much of a pause in between."

"Okay." His gaze went back to his feet as he started to move.

"Hey, I know I've got great boobs, but maybe you could try looking at my face instead." Sacha grinned.

"What? I wasn't!" Jessie's face turned a lovely shade of red.

Sacha threw her head back, laughing. "I was joking!" She looked up at him with a sly smile. "Of course you can look at my boobs."

Jessie's jaw dropped. He looked at Dane, who was trying hard not to laugh.

"Come on, I'm having fun with you." Sacha playfully patted his chest.

"You'll get used to her," Dane said, amused. Sacha's way of relaxing people was to flirt. He had seen it all before. He wasn't bothered—if she was going to cheat on him, she'd hardly do it right in front of him now, would she?

"I think he could do with another drink." Sacha made her way to the fridge to retrieve some more beers. She topped up her glass while she was at it. "You gotta try not to think about it too much, and just feel it. Here, I'll show you." She put their drinks down and grabbed his hand, placing it on her hip. "Feel the movement of my hips." She slowly went through the steps, accentuating the hip movement for him. To her glee, his eyes never left her hips. "It's just like at the pub."

"Okay, I think I got it now." He took up the closed position again and started to move."

"Good!"

"You wanna try it to the music?" Dane asked, flicking through the playlist on the iPod.

"Good idea. I'll count you in." She waited for the music to start. "Ready?" He nodded. "Okay. Five, six, seven, eight."

Jessie had great timing; normally one of the hardest things to teach. Sacha was right in her assumption—he had potential.

"You're doing great! Now try sliding your right arm down hers, to an open position," said Dane. Jessie obliged. "Now if you want to turn her, you raise your hand on the hip step, that's her signal that she will be beginning to turn."

"Okay."

"Not too high, just slightly above my head." Sacha corrected his positioning before turning herself.

"You can turn me in either direction, just use the opposite hand to signal."

Jessie did a few basic steps before attempting to lead her through some turns. He was picking it up quickly.

"Are you sure you haven't done this before?" Sacha asked. "You're very good."

"Ah, thanks. Fast learner I guess." He chuckled.

"And he's got a great teacher." Dane gestured towards Sacha.

"*Teachers*. You guys are awesome," Jessie said. "You couldn't give me another demo, could you?"

"Yeah, of course. Any excuse to dance with my lady." Dane selected what song he wanted before offering his hand to Sacha. Taking full advantage of Jessie watching, she decided to play it up and make it as sexy as she could. She wrapped her arms around Dane's neck, her body pressed in close. Any chance she got, she would roll her hips in Jessie's direction. When Dane turned her so that her back was up against him, she slowly writhed her body up and down, holding eye contact with Jessie as she did so.

"That was hot!" Jessie clapped with enthusiasm. "You gotta show me how to do that!"

"Stick with us and we will." Sacha winked, as she ran her hand down his arm. "We can show you *all* the tricks."

Several drinks later, Sacha and Dane had shown Jessie the basic salsa and bachata steps—he really was a fast learner. The more drinks he had, the more he loosened up, and the more Sacha put her skills to use.

She was careful not to be too obvious in front of Dane, not that he would notice—she flirted with other men all the time and he never batted an eye. She had to play this one smart though. Jessie was Dane's friend. She would have to work on him slowly, until he could no longer resist her. It would happen. Eventually. She always got what she wanted.

"Guys, you have been fantastic, but I really should be going," Jessie said.

"Aww, you sure? We were just getting started. You can always crash here, eh babe?" Sacha pouted.

"Thanks, maybe next time." He smiled. "I'll just call a taxi."

"Sure thing, mate. Phone's up there." Dane pointed to the kitchen wall. "I think the number's on the fridge. Hang on." He staggered over, staring at the various magnets cluttering the front of the fridge. Grabbing one shaped like a car, he held it up, triumphant. "Here 'tis," he slurred.

"Thanks." Jessie made his call and gathered his things, ready to leave. They walked him to the door. Sacha held her arms out to him.

"Bring it in. We're huggers here." She pulled him down to meet her, so she could wrap her arms around him tightly. Her face in the crook of his neck, she brushed her lips lightly against his skin—soft enough that it wasn't obvious, but that he would question whether it had happened or if he'd imagined it. She pulled away, catching his eye. "Will we be seeing you in class?"

He held her gaze for a beat. "You know? I think you will. I had so much fun tonight."

"Yeah, me too." She smiled sweetly.

"We should do it again nex' week!" Dane chuckled. "It was good ta see ya again, man. I'm glad you came."

"Yeah, me too. Flick me a text when class is on, and I'll be there. I think it's fair to say I'm hooked now." He grinned, looking over his shoulder towards the road. "Sounds like my ride is here. Thanks again, guys." He jumped down the steps and jogged down the drive, giving a wave before climbing into the taxi.

"That went well," Sacha said as she closed the door.

"It sure did." Dane circled his arms around her waist, kissing her cheek. "Thanks for making him feel welcome."

"Don't mention it." She smiled, turning to face him. "It was my pleasure."

Chapter 5

Rory sat back and looked over her creations. Tan square; her secret recipe that had been passed down from her grandmother to her mother, to her; chocolate-chip cookies, and a two-tiered red velvet cake with cream cheese frosting. Not bad for an afternoon's work, even if she did say so herself. She couldn't think of a better way to spend her Sunday afternoon than cooking up a storm. She was more at home in her kitchen than anywhere else in the world.

She carefully manoeuvred the red velvet onto a cake stand, covering it with its glass lid so Maddi would see it when she came home. It was her favourite flavour, and Rory really wanted to cheer her up. She hadn't been herself since the break-up with Ty.

They hadn't been together long, but she had been smitten with the guy. Poor thing was devastated when he told her he was moving away and thought it best if they saw other people. Translation, "I want to sleep around."

It was week two of heartbreak city, and Rory was doing everything in her power to keep her best friend's spirits up. Every day seemed to be a little better than the last.

The two had been friends since the age of three. Rory had watched as another kid had made it their priority to pick on the new girl. After Maddi had been shoved by said kid, Rory had stepped in; if there was one thing she couldn't stand, it was a bully. She had taken an instant dislike for anyone who preyed on weaker/smaller people than themselves. It had become somewhat of a mission for her to stand up for the 'under-dogs' of the school yard.

Maddi and Rory had been thick as thieves ever since that day in kindergarten. Complete opposites of each other—sweet, shy girl Maddi, with her locks of golden curls, and confident, tom-boy Rory, with her peroxide-blonde pixie cut—together, they were the complete package. You couldn't have one without the other.

When they had reached high school, and started getting interest from guys, they had relied on each other's opinions. If they didn't pass the 'best friend test' then they were tossed aside. Some guys weren't so keen on the set-up, not wanting to have the 'third wheel' hanging around so much. Others tried to use it to their advantage, seeing if they could charm them into a threesome. Those guys never got very far.

As far as Maddi was concerned, sex was off the cards. She had been tempted, but there hadn't been anyone special who really made her feel that it was the right time. Until that day came, she would remain pure.

Rory on the other hand, was a little more open to things. She didn't sleep around, but if it felt right, then she was up for anything. Except a threesome with her best friend, of course.

She admired Maddi's self-control. It wasn't one of Rory's strongest qualities. She tended to get caught up in the heat of the moment.

Somehow, Maddi was able to stop herself from going too far. It was quite impressive. Rory had witnessed the frustration on Ty's face as Maddi sent him packing each night, all hot and bothered. The poor guy. You couldn't fault him for trying though. Maddi was gorgeous. She was one of those girls who was oblivious to her looks. She didn't even have to try. Long, lithe legs, bouncing blonde curls, piercing blue eyes and full pouty lips. She was tall and slender, but not without curves. She even woke up fresh-faced every morning; unlike Rory, who would have hair sticking out in all directions and eye liner smeared down her cheeks. Yep she certainly was a sight to behold.

To top it all off, Maddi was the sweetest, most down-to-earth girl you would ever meet. She really did have everything going for her. It was no wonder so many girls were threatened by her. If they only took the time to get to know her though, they would fall in love with her too.

Rory hung up her apron and switched the jug on to make herself a coffee. She put a slice of tan square on a saucer, then added a cookie too. She grabbed her favourite cup down from the cupboard and scooped in some coffee and sugar before getting the milk from the fridge. Hearing the front door open, she smiled.

"You're just in time. Wanna cuppa?"

"Sure!"

"Ooh, somebody's happy." She spun around to face her friend. Maddi had a huge grin plastered on her face. "Alright, spill."

"I've found something I think will be fun for us to do."

"Sounds intriguing. Tell me more."

"Salsa!"

"Salsa?"

"Salsa." She nodded. "I saw a poster advertising this studio called Latin Flava. They have these free beginners' classes starting tonight. You wanna go?" She clasped her hands together as if praying. "Please!" To really drive it home, she batted her eyelashes and pouted her lips.

Rory couldn't help but laugh. This was the most enthusiastic she had seen Maddi since Ty left. "Of course! Sounds like fun."

Maddi clapped her hands gleefully. "Yay! Thanks so much!" She raced over to hug her friend. "Do you think we need to dress up?" She pulled away, clutching Rory's shoulders. "What are we going to wear?"

"Whoa there, Nelly, it's just a class. I doubt they expect us to dress all Latina." Maddi's face dropped like a child who'd had their favourite toy taken away. Rory quickly added, "But I'm sure we could spice it up a bit. We'll have a fashion montage like they do in the movies. I'm sure we can find something hot to wear."

"Thanks, Rory. I really need this. And I've always wanted to try it. It's so sexy!" She wiggled her hips towards the kitchen then spied the baking on the bench. "Is that? Is that red velvet cake I see?"

Rory nodded with a grin. "All for you."

"Oh my God, you are the best friend a girl could have!" She flung her arms around her friend before carefully lifting the lid, running her finger through the frosting and popping it into her mouth. "Mmm… so good!"

"Okay, how about, we have a coffee and some cake, and then we can do our montage." She took a bite of her tan square.

"Deal," Maddi said, as she sliced herself a sizeable chunk of cake.

Chapter 6

After trying on every outfit in their wardrobes, Rory and Maddi finally decided on something to wear to their first-ever salsa class. Rory had opted for sheer black tights and denim shorts over the top, with a cute crop top that hung off her shoulder. A myriad of silver bracelets adorned her arms and hoop earrings for her ears.

Maddi, not wanting to draw too much attention to herself, had gone for some black leggings with cut-outs down the sides, and a tight pink singlet. Going for a more simplistic look, she chose to wear just the one leather bracelet and matching necklace.

They walked the few blocks down to where the studio was situated, a nervous excitement between them. Rory was secretly hoping for some hot guys to be there. As far as she was concerned, there was nothing hotter than a guy who could dance. She was always drawn to them when they were out at the pubs. Of course, they were normally there to dance anyway, so if anyone was going to catch her eye, it would be someone on the dancefloor.

A hot dancer would be a good distraction for Maddi too. Something to get her mind off Ty.

She wasn't disappointed. The studio, to her surprise, was filled with guys. She had expected to see a room full of women and barely any men, but it seemed to be the opposite. There were more than a few potentials in there. She looked at Maddi with a gleam in her eye.

"Look at how many men there are," she whispered loudly, a grin spreading across her face. "I wonder how many were dragged here by girlfriends, and how many are here to pick up chicks." She craned her neck, checking out every last corner of the studio.

"Wow, there's a lot more people here than I expected," Maddi said, wiping her hands down her thighs. "I didn't realise how popular it is."

"Well, *Dancing with the Stars* has probably had a hand in that."

"Yeah, I didn't think about that."

"You okay? You still wanna stay?"

Maddi took a deep breath. "Yeah, I wanna stay. It'll be good for me. I haven't been to a dance class in years."

"I'll be right here by your side, bumbling my way through." Rory gave her hand a squeeze. "Come on, let's go sign up."

They walked up to the counter where a bubbly redhead took down their details. Class would be starting in five minutes, and she pointed them to the open area in the centre to find a spot to stand. Lines were beginning to form already, so they tagged onto the end of one near the front.

The redhead walked up to the stage and turned her headset on.

"Welcome, everyone, to the free beginners' salsa class! I'm Rachel, and I will be your instructor this evening." She smiled, her eyes lighting up. "Tonight, I'm going to show you some merengue moves which will get you dancing and shifting your weight properly for the salsa steps that we'll do at the end of the class. Don't worry if you haven't got a partner, we will move around the circle, that way everyone gets to have a go, and you will actually learn faster." She paused, pushing some buttons on a remote she had in her pocket. The studio was filled with music. "This is a merengue beat." She started to move her feet. "Left, right, left, right." She switched the music off again. "Not so daunting, is it?" She grinned, looking around at the eager faces. "Okay, so the movement is like climbing stairs. Left, right, left, right. Now, ladies, I know it's tempting to try and push those hips out like you see the pros do, but you will get into bad habits if you force it. Just focus on your feet first, and the hips will follow." She began marching on the spot. "This is how it should look."

"This is fun!" Rory whispered.

"I know! I love it already!"

"Alright, everyone, I'm going to put a song on for a warm-up. Just follow me!" Rachel turned the sound up and started calling out different directions for them to step in. Before long, they were all keeping in time and there were smiles all around.

"Okay, I want you to make a circle now. Grab a partner, or if you don't have one then you can slot yourself into the gaps." She waited as everyone began to organise themselves into a rough circular shape. Moving into the centre of the circle, she grabbed one of the spare bodies to partner her. She showed everyone how to get into a closed position and got them doing some basics on the spot. "Alright, now high five and moving on to the next person!" she called out.

There was light chatter as people introduced themselves to their new partners. Slowly, Rachel showed them a simple merengue combo, breaking down each step. They rotated around the circle after each section of the move.

"Alright, we'll do it one more time slowly, and then we'll try it to music. I'll get you all to move around once more."

Maddi stepped up to her new partner.

"Hi, I'm Jessie. Is this your first class too?" He smiled down at her.

"I'm Maddison… Maddi, and yeah it is. Does it show?" She giggled, her nerves getting the better of her.

"Not at all, Maddison Maddi. You make it look so easy!"

"Thanks." She blushed. "I've always wanted to try it."

"Well, it suits you." He pulled her in to the closed position, waiting for Rachel's instructions. Maddi looked over at Rory, who was giving her the thumbs up and mouthing, *Go for it! He's hot!* She stifled her giggle as she turned back to Jessie with colour in her cheeks.

"Friend of yours?" he asked, smirking as he watched Rory.

"Ah, yeah. I dragged her along with me. Excuse her. She doesn't know the meaning of the word subtle."

Jessie laughed. "You've got that right. I'm flattered, actually."

"Oh?"

"Well, clearly she thinks I'm worthy of you. I'd be lying if I said I didn't find you attractive." He smiled easily, his eyes searching hers.

"Oh, um, thanks?" She giggled again. "I don't really know what to say."

Jessie chuckled. "You don't have to say anything, let's just dance." He winked at her, before pulling her through the move as if he'd been doing it all his life.

"Now who's the natural?" she asked.

"I've got friends who dance. They showed me a few things in the weekend. They were meant to be meeting me here tonight, but I haven't seen them yet."

"You're so lucky! I'm definitely going to have to join classes I think."

"Yeah, it's pretty fun, eh? I'm sure Sacha and Dane wouldn't mind an extra person to teach, ya know, if you wanted to join me some time."

"Oh, ah, yeah, maybe."

"It's okay, I'm not a serial killer or anything." He winked again.

"It's not that. I'm just not really, ready for…" She stopped herself, pulling her lip between her teeth, worried she'd gotten the wrong idea.

"Oh no, of course, I mean, we just met. I just thought, ya know, you dance really nicely, and I'd like to dance with you some more. No pressure."

"Thanks… Um… Can I think about it?"

"Yeah of course." He spun her out, sending her on to the next guy in the circle. "See you around, Maddison Maddi." He grinned.

After class, Rory came bounding up to Maddi.

"So?"

"So what?"

"So, did you ask him out?"

"What? I just met the guy!" She laughed. "He did ask me to practise with him though," she said, as she turned to grab her gear, trying to hide the smile on her face.

Rory squealed. "That's awesome! He's so gorgeous!"

"Yeah, maybe a little," she teased. "Alright, maybe a lot."

"Speak of the devil," Rory said, making herself scarce.

"Hey, ah, here's my number, in case you want to go over some stuff." Jessie handed Maddi a piece of paper. "Ya know, if you want." He ran his hand through his hair before putting his jacket on. "It was nice to meet you."

"Yeah, you too. And thanks." She smiled.

"Hey, there you are! I thought you guys were coming to class with me?" Jessie said as he spied Sacha and Dane walking through the door.

"You didn't tell him, did you?" Sacha frowned at Dane.

"I must've forgot, sorry. We don't normally come to the free beginners'. We thought you'd probably want to stay on for the next class though."

"Oh, okay. Will I be able to do it?"

"Of course, babe, we wouldn't suggest it otherwise." Sacha winked at him as she shrugged her jacket off. She sat down, retrieving her dance heels from their bag. "It's still a beginners' class, just a few lessons in. I'll talk to Rachel and square you a spot."

"Thanks, Sacha." He smiled warmly.

Dane pulled him aside and asked, "So, did you pick up?" He grinned. Jessie laughed, kicking his toe into the floor but not saying anything. "You did, didn't you?" Dane slapped him on the back. "Smooth operator, you are."

"Bit of a stud, are we?" Sacha drawled. She stood up and touched his arm. "Don't be too hasty."

"Hey, us guys have needs." Dane smirked, planting his hand on her backside for emphasis.

"Don't I know it," she sneered.

"I'm not in any rush. She just moves well, and I thought it might be good to practise with her. I'm picking she won't be without a partner for long."

"That good, huh? You wanna snap her up then, mate."

"Yeah, that's what I was thinking. I already gave her my number."

"Well, until then, you are more than welcome to use me as a practise buddy," Sacha purred, rubbing his arm.

"Thanks, Sacha."

"Best way to fast-track your dancing. She'll whip you into shape, no worries."

"And you don't mind me stealing your girl all the time?"

"Mate, of course not. I trust you."

Chapter 7

"Oh my God! That was so much fun!" Maddi danced around Rory as they walked back home. "I'm definitely going back for more. How 'bout you? Did you like it? What did you think?"

"Yeah, it was pretty cool. I could go again." She smiled. "On one condition."

"Anything!"

"You have to ask Jessie out." She grinned, a mischievous glint in her eye.

"Oh, so you're gonna play it that way, are you?" Maddi smirked. "Well, joke's on you, I was already thinking about doing that anyway." She stuck her tongue out at Rory.

"Wait, what?" Rory stopped her. "You're gonna do it?"

"Mmm. Maybe."

"That's a yes."

"No, it's a maybe."

"It's a yes." Rory giggled. "You like him," she sang as she began skipping along the road, dragging Maddi with her.

"Alright, alright. Maybe I do like him." She held up her finger and thumb. "A little." She beamed. "He *was* pretty hot. And man, he could move."

"Mmhmm. The perfect combination. I mean, you know what they say about men who can dance."

"Um, no, what?"

Rory waggled her brows. "Got moves on the dancefloor, got moves in the bedroom."

Maddi shook her head, laughing. "Of course they do."

"Hey, they don't call it the horizontal tango for no reason."

"All sorted." Sacha smiled at Jessie as she sauntered back over. "She is happy for you to join in tonight and for the rest of the term if you like."

"That's brilliant! Thanks, Sacha."

"Don't mention it," she said. "You ready to get your dance on?" She grabbed his hand and dragged him out to the dancefloor. "We'll have a little warm-up while everyone is getting ready."

Wrapping her arms around his neck and pulling herself in nice and close, she waited for his lead. They swayed side-to-side to get the beat, then he started to move his feet.

"Good. Don't be afraid to hold me tighter. You won't break me, I promise." She winked. "I need to feel your leads, so really hold me." His grip tightened. "Now use your hand to direct me. Put pressure on your palm to move me this way, then with your fingertips, to move me that way."

Jessie did as she asked. He carefully manoeuvred her around the floor, while she writhed her hips against his, all the while, staring deep into his eyes.

"Everybody, gather round! Class is about to start!" Rachel called out as she made her way to the stage once more. Jessie blinked, breaking his gaze and stepping away from Sacha. His cheeks flushed red.

"You look like you're getting the hang of it," Dane whispered, as he joined them.

"Ah, yeah, I think so," Jessie stammered, suddenly feeling very self-conscious. He hadn't meant to get so caught up while dancing with Sacha, she was just so mesmerizing. The way she moved, the way she looked at him; like he was the only one in the room. If he didn't know any better, he'd swear she was flirting with him. But that wasn't possible, she was his best friend's girl for Christ's sake.

Sacha was pleased. She had seen the look in his eyes when they danced and when he pulled away. She had him. Now to reel him in.

"I thought maybe I could dance with Jessie tonight, while you dance with some of the other beginners. Share our knowledge around." Sacha smiled at Dane. A good stroke to the ego never hurt.

"Good idea. We can be good Samaritans for the night." He chuckled. "He's doing really well, don't ya think?" He nodded at Jessie.

"Yeah, he is." She looked over at him, smiling sweetly as she gave him a little wave. "Maybe while you're having a dance with the others, you could suss out a good match for him."

"Hmm. Not a bad idea. Though I think he was keen on dancing with that girl from earlier."

"Yeah, but we don't even know if she's going to stick around. Plus, he's new to this. You can get a better feel for their talents."

"Yeah, you're probably right. I'll do my best."

"Thanks, baby." Sacha gave his arm a squeeze before brushing past him and over to Jessie. "Hey, handsome, you're dancing with me tonight." She took him by the hand. He laughed uncomfortably.

"No, really, you don't have to give me special treatment. I can move around the circle like everyone else. You go dance with Dane," he offered.

"Nope. It's a done deal. You're stuck with me." She ran her tongue over her lips.

"Oh, okay then." He sighed, shuffling his feet.

"Don't be too excited there, cowboy," she said, sarcasm oozing.

"Sorry. It's not you. I just don't want Dane to get the wrong idea, ya know?"

"And what wrong idea would that be?" she whispered, looking up at him through her long lashes.

"What? I mean… ya know, like… I was into you, or something," he stammered, his cheeks turning a brighter shade of red.

"So, you're not into me?" she asked, pushing her hips into his and stroking her hand along his neck.

"I… ah." He pulled back a bit. "Of course I am. Look at you." Sacha beamed at that. "But that doesn't mean I'm going to act on it. You're my best friend's girl."

She pulled his head closer to hers, her lips brushing his ear. "What if I want you to act on it?"

"What?"

"You heard me. We'd be good together."

"But, Dane?" Jessie pulled back, frowning.

"What about him? He's a big boy, he'll get over it."

"What?"

"It's not really working out between us. It's run its course. He's not what I want anymore. And *you* are." She flicked her tongue into his ear before pulling away.

"… and cross body lead into a right turn for the ladies!" Rachel's voice came over the speaker.

Sacha led herself through the combo, letting her proposal settle with Jessie. His eyes kept darting between her and Dane, as if weighing up his options.

"Less thinking. More dancing." She grabbed his chin, making him look at her. "Focus."

"Easier said than done. You just dropped a bombshell on me."

"Don't act like it hadn't crossed your mind. I've seen the way you look at me."

"Again, I had no intentions of doing anything about it."

"Well, now I'm offering you a chance to get what you want. You know it would be good." She licked her lips provocatively.

"I don't doubt that. But Dane's my friend. I can't do it to him."

"Okay, I get it. You're loyal, I like that. But don't expect me to give up. I can be *very* convincing when I want to be." She rubbed up against him before spinning herself out to join the rest of the circle.

"You're looking awfully smug," Dane said, giving Sacha a gentle squeeze as she spun into his arms.

"Just thinking about how well Jessie is doing." She looked across the room to where he was. "He's quite the natural."

She watched as he tried to distract himself. It was obvious he was trying to avoid her; clearly, she had gotten inside his head, and she loved it.

"He's got you to thank for it. You've been really good with him." He pulled her in tightly, tilting her chin upwards. "Thank you." He bent down, kissing her sweetly.

"Anything for my baby," she cooed.

Dane smiled, rubbing his nose with hers. "I love you," he whispered.

"Back at ya," she offered, reaching up to plant a kiss on the tip of his nose. "Shall we go?" she asked, risking a glance around him to see if Jessie was watching.

To her delight, he was. A fire danced across his eyes before he looked away, brooding. She smiled to herself, satisfied with her evening's work. It wouldn't be long before he was hers.

"Sure. I'll just go say bye to Jessie." He trotted towards his friend.

Sacha turned to retrieve her shoes and jacket, all the while, keeping her eyes on the interaction between the two.

"Hey, man." Dane clapped his hand with Jessie's. "We're about to head off."

"Oh, okay cool. Thanks for coming down."

"Anytime. You're doing really well, ya know. We were just talking about you." Dane motioned towards Sacha. She wiggled her fingers in the air.

"Thanks, man. I'm really enjoying it."

"You should come around again this week, we can go over some more stuff."

"Oh, I don't know. I don't wanna impose…"

"Mate. You're not imposing. We live for this stuff." He nudged him with his elbow. "Come on, it'll be fun."

Jessie stole a glance at Sacha. "Yeah, of course. Sounds great." He gave a tight smile.

"Excellent! We'll see ya later then." Dane slapped his friend on the back before walking back to Sacha.

"Ready to go, babe?" He offered his hand.

"Sure am." She let him pull her up, lacing his fingers with hers as they walked out of the studio.

Jessie watched them walk out together, holding hands, bodies pressed close. He hated himself for feeling jealous. Dane was his friend. He shouldn't even be thinking about Sacha that way, but now that she'd revealed herself to him, he couldn't get her out of his head. Damn her!

She was enjoying watching him squirm too, he could see it in her eyes. They sparkled whenever she caught him looking at her. He had tried so hard not to, but something about her drew him in. It was like he was under a spell.

He heard her voice ringing in his head. *"He's not what I want anymore. And* you *are."*

He shook his head. She was playing with him. She had to be. He had just watched her kiss Dane.

And leave with him.

It couldn't be real.

He had to get her out of his head. He couldn't fall for his friend's girl. It just wasn't right.

Chapter 8

Maddi spent the next few days practising the steps she had learned. Every time a song with an eight count came on the radio, she would break into dance. The rest of her spare time was spent YouTubing salsa moves. She was hooked.

A timetable of all the classes available hung on the fridge for all to see. Maddi checked it every day, even though she practically had the thing memorised. She had circled all the beginner classes so that she didn't miss one. Tonight, there was another free one that she was wanting to go to.

She knew it would probably be the same moves repeated, but she didn't care, she just wanted to be there. It made her feel good. The music was so upbeat and happy that it was virtually impossible to stay in a bad mood.

It was an added bonus that she happened to be good at it.

And then, of course, there was Jessie. She knew it was silly to think that she had fallen for him after their brief encounter. No, he just made her feel good about herself. Made her feel as though she was worth the effort. It was a nice change.

Not that Ty had been a bad guy. He had just been very intent on getting into her pants, and every time she resisted, she saw the resentment in his eyes. She wasn't stupid, she knew it was why he left. It saddened her that he couldn't see past that—see that she was more than just a body. She knew she deserved to be treated better, but it still didn't stop it from hurting.

Salsa was the first thing to make her feel like her old self again after he'd left, and Jessie was a part of that.

She hadn't called him, even though Rory had been rather persistent. She figured he would be at the classes too, if he really was as keen as he said he was. It would be nice to have a dance partner to practise with though.

Rory was pleased to see her friend back to her happy, bubbly self again; even if she was being stubborn about Jessie. She'd never liked Ty, and Jessie seemed like a much better fit for Maddi. He seemed like a genuinely nice guy. It would be good for her to get back on the horse again. Nothing like a new love interest to ease a broken heart.

Rory had hoped to join Maddi at the next dance class to give her a much-needed push in the right direction, but duty called. She was a casual for a catering company and she couldn't turn down the chance to work. Maddi would just have to fend for herself this time.

"How do I look?" She came out, giving a twirl, her chiffon skirt taking flight.

"Ooh pretty!" Rory grinned. "Is that new?"

"It might be." Maddi giggled. "It was on sale and I couldn't resist it." She brushed her hands down the front of her skirt. "I fell in love with it. I thought it would look cool on the dancefloor."

"It's awesome, it really suits you." Rory dried her hands, walking around the counter to join her friend.

"I wish you were coming with me."

"I know, me too. But you know how much I love my job."

"Yeah, I know." Maddi smiled. "I'm just a little nervous going by myself."

"Are you kidding? You were amazing. You're gonna be just fine on your own." Rory placed her hands on Maddi's shoulders. "You and those hips were born for this."

"Thanks."

"Just promise me something."

Maddi rolled her eyes.

"Don't do that! You haven't even heard what I'm going to say!"

"Sorry. Go ahead, I'm listening."

"Promise me you will at least talk to him? You don't have to ask him out, just be friends if you'd rather. I just have this feeling he would be really good for you."

Maddi sighed. "Alright."

"Good." Rory beamed. "You'll thank me for it."

"Yeah, yeah." Maddi grinned. "Well, I guess I'd better head off. What time will you be home?"

"It's only a few hours so I should be home about nine. If you need me to be later though…" She winked. "Just flick me a text."

Maddi laughed. "Don't go getting ahead of yourself. I said I'd *talk* to him. I'm not about to jump his bones."

"We'll see." Rory grinned mischievously as she walked out the door.

Down at the studio, Maddi was standing quietly in the corner, trying to find a familiar face. She had been to plenty of dance classes as a child, but her confidence had waned somewhat over the years, and she wasn't as good at meeting new people as she used to be. Everyone seemed to be in groups already and she wasn't sure where she would fit in.

"You look lonely," Jessie whispered as he sidled up next to her.

"Oh, hey." She smiled, feeling her cheeks redden. "I was just thinking that I didn't recognise anyone here."

"Well, now you know me." Jessie chuckled. "But yeah, I guess this is a whole new group of people than the other night." He scanned the room. "Maybe we're the only insane ones who came back to repeat a basic beginners' class."

"Yeah, you're probably right." Her eyes sparkled as she let out a soft laugh. Jessie had a way of putting her at ease with only his presence.

"What do you say? Shall we team up tonight?" he asked, nudging her with his elbow.

Her lips curled into a smile. "Sure."

He grabbed her hand and led her out to the front of the studio. No one else had ventured away from the outer edges of the room, instead waiting for others to make the first move.

"Best spot in the class." He winked.

The chatter began to die down as Rachel took to the stage.

"Gather round, everyone! Make some rows and we'll rotate back to front so that you all get a chance to see." She began running over the same merengue moves they had done for a warm-up last time.

"Ready to look like pros?" Jessie whispered, winking. Maddi giggled.

"Hardly!"

"Compared to these newbies, we are." He grinned, taking her hand. "We got this."

The music started, and they ran through the warm-up before forming a circle. Jessie pulled her in to his side, making sure she stayed with him.

"Have you been practising?"

"Guilty. I can't help it! Every time I hear music, I find myself counting the beats to see if I can salsa to it." She laughed. "I think I may have an addiction."

"I know what you mean. I do the same thing." Jessie chuckled as he gave her a spin. "I think we have a problem."

"Hmm, you could be right. I wonder if there's a cure," Maddi joked. "Not that I want there to be. It's too much fun!" She rolled her body towards Jessie, his eyes widening.

"Where did you learn that?" he asked, a wide grin spreading across his face. "It looks *really* good."

Maddi beamed. "I used to dance when I was younger. That, and I may have been watching a bit of YouTube." She chewed her lip, looking up at Jessie.

"I'm obviously gonna have to do some of that too if I'm going to keep up with you."

"I seem to recall you having private lessons. I think you'll be fine."

"Yeah, I don't know how much longer I'll do those though. I mean it must suck teaching newbies when you've got your own stuff to practise."

"I guess. It's probably a nice change for them though. I'm sure they wouldn't offer to teach you if they didn't enjoy it."

"Yeah, you're probably right." He bent down to whisper, "It's more fun this way though." When he pulled back, his eyes glistened with mischief.

Maddi couldn't help but grin up at him. "Aww, you're sweet. It *is* pretty fun dancing with you."

"Why, thank you." Jessie smiled, a thoughtful look on his face. "I hope we can do this some more."

"Me too." She bit her lip, suddenly all too aware of their close proximity. He really was a good-looking guy.

It was still too soon though. Ty had only left three weeks ago, and she wasn't in any hurry to jump straight back into another relationship. Someone needed to remind the butterflies in her stomach of that though; they flittered about like crazy whenever Jessie looked at her with that lazy grin of his.

"You up for one more dance?" he asked, snapping her out of her thoughts.

"Huh? Oh, yeah sure," she said, pushing aside any feelings for him. "Lead away."

Chapter 9

After class, Rachel asked Maddi to join her for a chat. Jessie looked on with raised brows.

"Somebody's the teacher's pet," he joked.

"I doubt it. I'm probably in trouble. I haven't actually signed up for any classes yet. Maybe she wants to tell me not to come to the free classes if I'm not paying for the other ones." She frowned, running her hand through her hair.

"Are you serious? You won't be in trouble! She can't offer free classes and not have people come along. I bet she wants to tell you how good you are."

"I don't know."

"Maddi, listen to me. You. Are. A. Star. Everyone can see it." He motioned around the room. "You can dance circles around anyone here."

Maddi sighed. "I hope you're right."

"I know I am." He ruffled her hair. "You just need to believe in yourself, kid."

She batted his hand away, laughing. "Enough of the 'kid' talk, thanks." She grabbed her gear and rocked back and forth on her toes. "I guess I should go see what she wants."

Jessie put his hands on her shoulders, turning her to face Rachel. "Go get 'em!" He gave her a gentle push. She stepped forward, peering back over her shoulder at him. *Go*, he mouthed, waving her on.

She took a deep breath and walked with more confidence than she felt.

"Rachel? You wanted to see me?"

"Yes, Maddi, isn't it?" She smiled, bringing a rush of relief to Maddi.

"Yeah, ah, yes, it is."

"I couldn't help but notice how fast you are picking up the moves. I wanted to let you know that we have a girls' dance troupe if you're interested in some solo work."

"Oh, really? That sounds great."

"Yeah, it's a small group, but we get together on Saturday mornings for an hour or two. We're working on a new routine so it's the perfect time to join." She smiled. "I think you would fit in really well."

"Wow, I wasn't expecting that at all. Um. I'd love to join."

"Great. Here are the details," she said, handing her a card. "If you have dance shoes then wear those, otherwise I have some spare pairs that would probably fit you."

"No, no, I've got some I can wear. Will jazz shoes be okay?"

"They'll be fine. If you decide you want to pursue dance further, you'll need to get some heels, but we can look into that later." She looked down at her desk. "If you're interested, I could use some help behind the desk some nights. It would mean that you could watch the other classes and join in on some too, if you like. Free of charge."

"Seriously?"

"Yeah, if you're interested. I mean, I hope I'm not overstepping here."

"No, I'd love to help out! Any excuse to immerse myself in dance." She couldn't believe her luck. And to think, she had thought she was going to be told to leave.

"I'll let you get back to your friend, but we should catch up for a coffee one night. We can go over the timetable."

"Thanks so much, Rachel. Honestly, this means so much to me." She rummaged in her bag for a pen. "Here's my number, let me know when you want to meet up. I'm free anytime." She spun on her heels and skipped back to where Jessie was waiting.

"You look happy with yourself. I told you it was gonna be good news." He grinned.

"She wants me to join her dance troupe!" she said excitedly. "Can you believe it?" She bounced up and down, her cheeks flushed. She very nearly threw herself into his arms, she was so excited.

"Wow! That's better than good news, that's fantastic! Congratulations!"

"Thanks. I can't wait to tell Rory."

"Ah, yes, your really subtle friend. Where is she tonight?"

"Yes, that's the one." She laughed. "She had to work."

"So, you're going home by yourself?"

"Yeah, I only live around the corner though."

"Can I walk you? Just to make sure you get home safely?"

"Sure, that would be nice."

"Great." He offered his arm for her to grab onto. "Let's get you home."

They made their way out the door and down the stairs to the ground below. The lights of the surrounding stores and bars twinkled brightly, lighting their way. They walked in a comfortable silence, arm-in-arm, Maddi pointing out the direction of her house.

"You know, my friends live near here. The ones I was telling you about."

"Oh yeah? I've probably seen them around then. It's quite a busy wee area."

"I can see that. I guess having a shopping area so handy keeps it alive."

"Mmm," she agreed. "I like it. It's like having our own wee town inside this big city. Reminds me of home."

"You're not from here?"

"Well no, not really. I lived here when I was little, then my Dad got offered a job in a place much smaller than this. I moved back here earlier this year with Rory."

"Ah, I can see why you find it so daunting then." He smiled.

"Yeah, it takes a bit of getting used to."

"Well, I'm always just a text away if you ever need a friend."

"Thanks." She paused at her driveway. "This is me." She waved her arm towards her little house. "Did you want to come in for a coffee?"

"You know, I would like that." He nodded, following her up the steps.

She unlocked the door. "Rory?" she called out. Silence. "She must be still at work." She walked through to the kitchen and switched the jug on. "How do you have it?"

"Huh? Oh, just milk please," he answered as he wandered around the room, looking at the photos on the wall. "Is this you and Rory?" He pointed at a picture of two kids no more than four years old, covered in ice cream, with big grins plastered on their faces.

"It sure is. We've been friends a long time." She smiled, handing him his cup. "That was after a trip to the zoo. We had begged our parents for an ice cream the whole day."

"You look like little trouble-makers."

"Yeah, sometimes." She paused. "Well, Rory was anyway." She laughed.

"Why doesn't that surprise me?" He laughed with her.

"Hey, you hungry? Rory baked me a cake the other day and there's still some left."

"Ooh sounds good. I do love cake."

"Rory is like the best baker in the world. Seriously, you won't want any other after you try it."

"Wow, that's high praise. It must be pretty damn good. I can hardly pass up a slice of cake that'll make me forget all other cakes now, can I?"

Maddi grinned, bounding back to the kitchen. She pulled the cake out of the cupboard, holding it up triumphantly. "Ta da!" she sang.

He whistled. "Now, that's a cake."

"I know, right? I'm always telling her she should be making money out of this. It's like, her favourite thing to do." She cut two hefty slices, placed them on plates, and then ran her finger down the side of the knife to scoop off the icing before popping it into her mouth. Realising he was watching, she quickly removed her finger. "What? Don't judge until you've tried it. I bet you'd do the same." She waggled her finger at him.

"I don't know, you've talked it up a lot. I have high expectations now."

"And it will still blow those expectations out of the water. Trust me," she said knowingly. He grabbed his plate, and they sat on the couch.

"Alright, here goes." He took a large bite and as he began to chew, his face said it all. "Oh…My…God…" he mumbled.

"It's good, right?"

"That's the understatement of the year. It's the best cake I've ever eaten." He shovelled another piece into his mouth. "You know you've ruined all other cake for me now."

"I know." She smiled happily. "But it's so worth it." She tucked her legs underneath her as she too bit into the moist cake. They both sat there, nodding and chewing, unable to talk as they devoured the deliciousness.

"I think I just had a foodgasm," Jessie said, leaning back in his seat, rubbing his stomach. Maddi giggled.

"Yeah that happens a lot around here." She smirked. "I'll tell Rory she has a new fan."

"You do that. I'm gonna have to run home to burn this off."

"Like *you* need to worry about that."

"Oh yeah? Been checking me out, have you?" He chuckled.

"No!" Maddi's cheeks burned with embarrassment. "I mean…"

Jessie laughed. "It's okay, Maddi. I was just joking." He stood. "I really should get going though. I promised Dane I'd stop by after class."

"Oh, okay." Maddi stood and walked him to the door. "Well, thanks for the walk home."

"Anytime. Thanks for ruining cake for me."

"Anytime."

Chapter 10

Jessie walked the short distance to Dane and Sacha's, hoping their little encounter would be forgotten. If it had been up to him, he would have avoided going there at all, but Dane had been asking, and he couldn't keep putting it off any longer; not without it seeming suspicious.

Sacha had made it pretty clear that she intended on having him, no matter what the cost. Maybe if he told her he'd been with Maddi this evening, it would put her off, at least for a while. He knew that theirs was just a friendship, but Sacha didn't need to know that.

He let himself in through the back door.

"Hello?" he called out.

"In here!" Dane's voice came from the lounge.

"Hey there, handsome." Sacha sauntered out of the bathroom to his left, wearing only a towel.

Jessie's mouth went dry. "Oh, hey. Sorry, I didn't know you were in there," he said awkwardly, averting his eyes.

Sacha let out a sultry laugh. "You don't need to be embarrassed. You know I did this for you, baby," she purred, brushing herself up against him seductively.

"Come on, Sacha. I told you," he glanced down the hall, "it's not happening." He pushed past her, through to the lounge where Dane was seated.

"Where've you been, mate? I thought you were coming after class?"

"Yeah, sorry 'bout that, I should've text." He looked to see if Sacha was in earshot. "I was with that chick I was telling you about. Maddi."

"Oh yeah? Good for you, man!" He slapped his friend on the shoulder as he joined him on the couch.

"Yeah, I really like her," he said pointedly, watching Sacha as she walked through to the other room, a sour look on her face. "I walked her home and she invited me in for coffee."

"Nice." Dane drew the word out. "You should've brought her here for a dance."

"Yeah, maybe next time. I didn't wanna just invite her to your place unannounced."

"Hey, man, mi casa, su casa, you know that."

Jessie nodded, so far so good. Dane jumped to his feet.

"Right, wanna get started?"

"Sure." Jessie stood, removing his jacket and throwing it on the couch behind him. "What're we doing tonight?"

"Well, I thought seeing as you're taking classes for salsa, we could go over some more bachata. You seem to be getting the hang of it pretty quickly."

"Sounds good."

Dane pushed some buttons on a remote, turning the T.V. off and the stereo on. He had a playlist ready and waiting.

"Let's do a warm-up while Sacha is getting dressed." He began stepping sideways to the beat. "Once you've got that basic beat down, try switching it up a bit. Like this." He changed his footwork, adding a fast two step in place of the hip flick he had shown Jessie the first time.

Jessie watched, counting the beat in his head until he was sure he had it. He closed his eyes, concentrating.

"That's it!" Dane grinned. "You've got it. So you can flick between each of those steps in your basic partner work too. Once you get more comfortable, you can change it up even more."

"Sweet. I think this is enough for now though."

"Yeah, absolutely. Hey, babe. Look, I showed him a bit of flare to add," Dane said proudly as Sacha joined them.

"Yeah, I see that." She smiled, planting a kiss on his cheek. "You ready for me?" She turned to Jessie with a smirk.

"Ah, yeah, sure," he said casually, trying his best to remain calm. She certainly had a way of getting under his skin. The way she held his gaze with a knowing look, or the way she pursed her lips before speaking, the intoxicating smell of her perfume. Everything about her drew him in, no matter how hard he tried to fight it.

She stretched her arms up to wrap around his neck and pulled him in as close as she possibly could. Resting her forehead on his chest, she began to sway to the music, her body rubbing against him sensually.

Jessie swallowed. He had to get a grip. Putting his hands on her hips, he gently eased her body away slightly as he started to move. He was not going to let her make a fool of him in front of Dane.

Attempting to keep his cool, Jessie walked through the basics they had taught him previously, throwing in the new steps he had just learned. Sacha took every chance she could to pull herself back into his embrace, rolling her body in every seductive way imaginable. Flashes of her glistening body covered only in a towel kept popping into his mind. It took every ounce of his concentration to keep it professional.

"Mate, I don't know where your head is at, but keep it there. You're rocking out moves we haven't even shown you yet!" Dane stood watching them in awe. "That's amazing!"

"He sure is a natural," Sacha purred, her eyes locked on Jessie.

"It won't be long before he's teaching us!" Dane joked. "Oh, that reminds me, I was gonna give you a DVD with some moves on it, so you can practise at home."

"Oh, thanks, man, that'd be great."

"I'll just go grab it. I think it's in the bedroom." He jogged down the hall to their room.

Jessie dropped his arms from around Sacha's waist, taking a step back. She quickly followed him, her arms still curled around his neck.

"Where're you going?" She licked her full lips, pushing up against him. "You can't fight it, I know you want me," she whispered.

"Sacha, please," Jessie stammered. It was hard to think straight when she was so close to him. She took advantage of his weakness and, running her hands down his arms, she gripped his wrists, bringing his hands to rest on her behind.

"I'm yours, baby. You just have to say the word," she murmured in his ear, her breathe warm on his neck. "I can do things you've only dreamed of," she whispered before darting her tongue into his ear.

Jessie let out an involuntary moan.

"Found it!" Dane called as he padded back to the lounge. Sacha grinned up at Jessie, holding a finger to her lips.

"Shhhh," she said, winking. Turning her back to him, she met Dane in the doorway. "I was thinking, we should copy some of our music for him too," she said so innocently, as if she hadn't just been all over Jessie.

"Yeah, I was thinking that too. Don't suppose you have a USB stick on ya?" he asked Jessie, who stared blankly back. Dane waved his hand in front of his face. "Earth to Jessie." He grinned. "I think we've overloaded his brain."

"What? Sorry, yeah, I guess it has been a long night. Maybe I should head home for some shut eye."

"No worries, mate. Here, take this with you at least." He handed the DVD to him. "I'll upload some songs for you and give it to you next time."

"Thanks, Dane."

"Hey, what are friends for?"

Jessie managed a smile even though the guilt was eating him up inside.

Chapter 11

Maddi climbed the stairs to the studio bright and early Saturday morning. Her stomach was churning, a mixture of excitement and nervousness. She hoped the other girls liked her. It would be nice to have some friends at the studio.

Standing outside the door, she brushed her hands down her clothes, smoothing out any non-existent wrinkles. Taking a deep breath, she pushed the door open and cautiously stepped through.

Rachel was behind the desk and gave her a warm smile.

"Maddi, you made it." She waved her in, walking out to meet her. "Come, I'll introduce you to everyone."

The girls gathered in a circle, eager to see who the newcomer was.

"Alright, guys, I have a new dancer to join us." She smiled. "She's only been to a few classes, but I can see she has real potential. I'd like you to meet Maddi."

Maddi stepped forward, giving a little wave. Sacha folded her arms across her chest, pushed her hip out and raised her brow in interest. The other girls barely noticed, welcoming her with open arms.

"It's lovely to meet you all," Maddi said, her unease washing away as she peered at the group of smiling faces. "I can't wait to see what you've been working on."

"Pay close attention. We don't have time to break it down for you. We have a performance coming up in a few weeks," Sacha said abruptly. She spun on her heels and stalked across the room.

Maddi was taken aback. How had she gotten off on the wrong foot already? This girl didn't seem very happy to have her on board.

"Ignore her," the girl beside her whispered. She had red hair that floated about her pale face and a dusting of freckles over her nose. "She just gets territorial whenever a new girl comes along. She's kinda the leader of the pack."

"Oh, I thought Rachel was."

"Well, yeah, but she pretty much lets Sacha do whatever she likes." She stopped, lowering her voice even more. "I hope for your sake, you learn fast. Try to get as much as you can, and then after class I can show you some more. If you don't keep up, she'll make your life a living hell." She grinned. "Speaking from experience." She bounded over to the rest of the group, doing some final stretches before they got started.

Could this be the Sacha who is teaching Jessie?

"Let's go!" Sacha called out. The girls scattered into position. Once they were ready, Rachel pressed a button on her remote and the room was filled with music. The girls all spun into various poses before strutting to the front in a V shape. The choreography was tight, and Maddi was impressed.

When they had finished, she clapped eagerly.

"That was amazing!" she gushed. "You guys are great dancers."

"Yeah, we know. That's why we're here," Sacha said dryly. "Are you in or not?"

"Absolutely. Where do you want me?" She walked over to join them. Sacha pointed at a spot to the far right, furthest away from her. Maddi swallowed back the hurt she felt from having this girl she had only just met, treat her so rudely, and walked with her head held high to the spot she had been designated.

Rachel started the music again, and Maddi followed along as best she could, having only seen it once. The start was easy enough but the further they got into the choreography the more lost she became. Some of these moves she had never seen before today. She would have a lot of work to do to get up to scratch, but she was determined to prove her worth to Sacha.

"Not bad, newbie. You got a long way to go, though," Sacha said when the music stopped again.

"Ah, thanks? I'll get it, I just need to see it a few more times I think."

"Well you can sit and watch, or you can join in and just do it. Your choice," she said, turning back to the others. Maddi had the feeling she was being tested. She knew she would learn more by watching it again, but somehow, she didn't think Sacha would approve.

"You ready?" Sacha looked at Maddi. She nodded, taking her place.

They ran through the song another five times before taking a break. Maddi was puffed but exhilarated. She was slowly getting the hang of it.

She jogged to her bag, retrieving her water bottle and taking a long drink. The red head wandered over, taking a seat beside her.

"You're a fast learner. You'll fit in well." She smiled. "Sacha will warm up to you, don't worry. We all had to go through this in the beginning. She thinks she's God's gift," she joked. "She is a bloody good dancer though."

"Yeah, I like her style. She almost glides along the dancefloor. I bet she gets a lot of attention from the boys," Maddi said.

"Mmm, she does, but they all know she's with Dane. They're like the power couple of the dancing circle here."

"Oh yeah? I don't think I've met him yet."

"Stick around long enough and you will. They're everywhere." She took a swig of her own bottle. "How 'bout you? Any fella out there you can dance with?"

"No, not really. I mean, there's this one guy, Jessie. We've had a few good dances together, and I think maybe he likes me."

"Oooh hold onto him then. The good male dancers get snatched up pretty quick." She snapped her fingers.

"Good to know." Maddi smiled. It was nice to have a friendly face to talk to. "Have you got a dance partner?"

"Me? Nah, I just dance with anyone and everyone," she joked. "Bit of a social butterfly." She winked, nudging her with her elbow.

"Alright, enough chit chat, let's get back to work!" Sacha called, clapping her hands together. "We've only got two more practises before our show at Feeney's. We need to be flawless." She looked Maddi up and down. "Think you can master it by then, newbie?" She almost spat the last word, as if it left a horrible taste in her mouth.

"Yeah, I think I can have it down in time," Maddi answered, her chin raised in defiance. She walked over to her starting position. Rachel gave her a little nod of encouragement.

"From the top!" she said, pushing play.

The girls rehearsed for another hour straight, going over every little move with a fine-tooth comb. Maddi had to admit, Sacha had a good eye. She picked up on all the minor details that they were missing. No wonder she had the ego she did, she was a force to be reckoned with.

When they decided to call it quits, Maddi grabbed a quick drink before running over a few of the moves in the mirror. Rachel gave her a few pointers, but most of the moves she had down, it was just a matter of perfecting them.

The others had all taken off straight after class, leaving only Maddi and Sacha. She stood by with a critical eye, calling out commands.

"Raise your arms higher in the spin. Sharpen up your hand movements. Smaller steps. Were you paying attention at all?"

Maddi had had about all she could take for one day. She spun around to address her.

"What is your problem? You've done nothing but criticise me since I walked in." She stood, hands on hips, waiting for a response.

"*You're* my problem, newbie."

"What did I do to piss you off? I've done everything you've asked me to do!" She slapped her arms down to her sides, frustrated. "I don't know what you want from me," she said more quietly. Her burst of courage was starting to fade, and unease was settling in the pit of her stomach. "I'll just go." She walked to where she had left her bag. Sacha stuck her foot out as she was walking past. Maddi stumbled but regained her balance.

"Oops," Sacha said sarcastically.

"You did that on purpose."

"What you gonna do about it? Go crying to Jessie?"

"Jessie? That's what this is about?" Maddi asked, stunned. Of all the reasons for her attitude, this was far from what she had suspected.

"Yeah, that's what this is about."

"But, aren't you with Dane?" she asked.

"So what if I am? Jessie is mine, and you need to stay away," Sacha said, her voice full of menace.

"You're laying claim on both of them?" Maddi asked. She couldn't believe what she was hearing.

"You can have Dane for all I care, but Jessie is off limits. Got it?"

Even though they had only met that day, Maddi could tell Sacha was not to be messed with. There was something about her that told her she always got what she wanted. Maddi was not about to get stuck in the middle of a love triangle.

"Sure. No problem. He's all yours," she said, grabbing her gear. "You might wanna tell him that though."

Chapter 12

"So, I just had the weirdest conversation," Maddi announced as she walked through the door, dumping her bag in her room on her way past.

"Ooh do tell," Rory said, flicking the jug on in preparation for a chat.

"There was this girl at training, Sacha, she's kinda the big star of the group."

"Mmm."

"Straight away I could tell she had it in for me. She was real snarky and rude to me. I've never met anyone like her."

"Sounds like a bitch." Rory screwed her face up in disgust. "You want me to sort her out for you?"

Maddi laughed. "No, no, it's alright. I think I can handle her." She walked into the kitchen to start on the coffee. "I haven't even told you the weird part yet."

"Sorry, carry on."

"So, at the end of practise, I was going over some of the moves in the mirror and she just stood there, yelling at me. I called her on it and, get this… she told me to stay away from Jessie." She raised her brow and pursed her lips.

"What's up with that? I thought he was single?"

"That's the thing. I'm pretty sure he is. She's with this other guy, Dane. She was all 'back off, he's mine,'" she mimicked, snapping her fingers in front of her face.

"Seriously? What's her deal? Stringing her man along until a better one comes along? What a cow!" Rory said angrily. How dare she threaten her friend. "You sure you don't want me to sort her out? It would be my pleasure." She punched her fist into her hand.

"Believe me, it's tempting. But I'd rather leave them to it. Jessie and I are just friends, it's not like anything has happened," Maddi said, handing Rory a steaming cup of coffee.

"Still. It's not right. Surely Jessie can't be interested in someone like that."

"We don't really know him that well. And you haven't seen her. She's gorgeous. Petite with dark hair and pale skin. She's got this exotic beauty. And you should see her dance. She's amazing."

"Ah, have you looked in a mirror lately? Girl, you're hot as hell." Rory licked the tip of her finger and held it to her skin making a hissing sound. "Anyways, beauty means nothing when you have the personality of a wet rag."

Maddi just shrugged. She secretly hoped that Jessie would turn her down, but knew it was unlikely. Girls like Sacha don't get turned down.

Jessie and Dane were busy going over some men's footwork when Sacha came marching in from practise. She dropped her keys on the bench and threw herself on the couch, stretching her legs out.

"What are you two up to?" she asked.

"Thought I'd show him some shine steps, spice up his solo stuff," Dane said, leaning down to kiss her. "How was training?"

"Not bad. I met your *friend*, Maddi," she said, screwing her face up in disgust.

"Oh yeah?" Jessie had been so happy for Maddi when she was asked to join the group, it had never crossed his mind that Sacha would be there too. He hadn't wanted them to meet like that, not without him warning Maddi about her first.

"Yeah. She seems… nice enough, I guess. Not exactly who I would have picked for you."

"What is that supposed to mean?" he asked.

"She just seems so… plain." She tucked a stray hair behind her ear, looking up at him through her dark lashes.

"They can't all be stunners like you, babe," Dane said, winking. He made his way into the kitchen to pour himself a glass of water. "Want one?" he asked Jessie, holding the glass up.

"Nah, I'm good. Thanks though." He turned his back on Sacha and went over the moves Dane had shown him.

"Do we have anything to eat?" Sacha asked over her shoulder. "I'm starving."

"I'll have a look." Dane went to the fridge. After staring into its depths for several minutes he declared it to be bare. "I can run down to the shops and grab some ham and salad for sandwiches if you like, babe."

"Would you? That would be great. Maybe some eggs too."

"Of course, my love. You guys can carry on without me." He grabbed his wallet and walked to the door. "Back soon!"

Sacha turned her attention to Jessie. She watched the muscles moving under his shirt as he practised. Her eyes wandered appreciatively up and down the rest of his body.

"Looking good, baby," she purred.

"Don't," Jessie snapped.

"Don't what?" she said innocently.

"You know what."

Sacha stood up, moving closer. "I'm not sure what you mean. Don't do this?" She ran her hand down his back, pressing her body against him. "Or this?" She snaked her other hand around his middle, finding her way under the waistband of his jeans. Jessie grabbed her hand, pulling it away.

"I said don't," he stated, less convincingly. She pouted.

"I know you don't mean that." She walked around to face him, trailing her hand around his shoulders and up his neck to rest at the nape. "I know you want me too," she whispered, standing on her toes to kiss his neck. She could feel his body responding which made her want him even more. She began to kiss and lick her way up his neck, gently pulling his face down to meet hers.

Jessie hated that his body was reacting to her touch, but he couldn't fight it anymore. She was so damn sensual. "Sacha," he said, his voice hoarse.

"Jessie," she breathed. She nibbled his lip, wanting to draw it out. Looking at him with hooded eyes, she pressed her lips to his.

With a growl, Jessie gave in, wrapping his arms around her waist and lifting her into his arms. She swung her legs around his middle, pulling them in tight. She needed to be as close to him as possible. She had thought of nothing more than this moment since that first night at Feeney's. It was better than she had imagined.

Jessie collapsed on the couch, taking her with him. She pulled her top over her head, grinning at him.

"I knew you wanted me too." She crushed her lips to his once more, rocking slowly in his lap, tormenting him. Her hands found the buttons on his shirt and started ripping at them, desperate to touch him. She arched her back as he began to kiss down her neck, tasting her. She sighed.

His hands gripped her behind, pulling her flush with his body. She ran her hands up his neck and cupped his jaw, bringing his mouth back to hers.

"What the fuck?" Dane dropped the bags of food he had been carrying. His hands balled into fists.

"Jesus, Dane!" Jessie sat forward, lifting Sacha from his lap. He stood, raking his hand through his hair.

"It's not what it… Shit. I'm so sorry. I don't know what came over me."

"Sit. Down," Dane demanded. "I go out for five minutes, and I come home to find you fucking my missus? What kind of a friend does that?"

"We weren't fucking," Sacha said, holding her hands up and inspecting her nails as if it was an ordinary day.

"Close enough," he spat, turning his attention back to Jessie. "Do your damn shirt up!"

Jessie looked down, fumbling with his buttons.

Dane began pacing. "How long?" he demanded, waving a finger between the two of them. "How long has this been going on?"

"This is the first time, I swear," Jessie said, holding his hands up, palms out. "Jesus, I'm so sorry, Dane."

"Save it." He continued pacing. "After everything I've done for you. This is how you repay me?"

"I never meant for this to happen."

"Oh no, of course not. She just slipped and fell into your lap without any goddamn clothes on!"

"Dane…" Sacha started.

"Don't. I thought you loved me." He looked at Sacha, angry tears in his eyes.

She had the decency to look ashamed. "I know. I'm sorry."

It wasn't the response he had expected. "You're sorry I thought that, or you're sorry you got caught out?"

"Both, I guess," she said, holding his stare defiantly. "We were never going to be a forever thing."

Dane couldn't believe what he was hearing. Had she been toying with him this whole time? Was it all just a game to her?

"Well, I guess we both had different views of what *this* was," he said, before walking out the door, slamming it behind him.

Chapter 13

"Shit!" Jessie stood up, pacing. "Shit!"

"Calm down. He's a big boy, he'll get over it," Sacha said, stretching her arms above her head.

"Are you serious?" he asked incredulously. "Don't you feel any remorse? You just broke his heart!"

"I think you had a hand in that too, don't you?" Sacha smirked.

"Yeah. I know. I'm an arsehole." He rubbed his hand across his face. "Goddamn it! I'm such a shitty friend." He pounded the counter with his fist. Sacha sighed.

"Don't be so dramatic. He *will* get over it. I promise." She joined him at the bench, running her hand down his back soothingly.

"Please don't," he murmured.

"I'm not coming on to you. I was *trying* to console you." She touched his face, turning him to look at her. "I *am* sorry you got stuck in the middle of this." She peered up at him. "I know you probably think I did it on purpose, but I didn't mean for him to find out this way. I would've ended it with him eventually." She took a breath. "Can you forgive me?"

Jessie let out a long breath. "Of course I can. It wasn't exactly one-sided. I just…" He shrugged. "Dane was my friend. I should never have let it get that far. I should've had more self-control."

"But you do like me, don't you?"

"You know I do." He cupped her face in his hands. "More than I'd like to admit."

Sacha smiled at that. For a second there, she thought she may have lost him.

"We should probably get out of here before he gets back. I doubt he's going to want to see us anytime soon."

"About that." Sacha wrung her hands together, hoping he would agree to what she was about to propose. "I couldn't stay with you, could I?" She peered up at him through her lashes. "Just for a little while. I don't really have anywhere else to go."

"I don't know. Is that really a good idea, considering?" He waved his hand around the room. "It's not going to look good, us shacking up straight after. He'll think we planned this whole thing."

She nodded, lowering her eyes. "I know. I wouldn't ask, I just don't have anyone else I can turn to." She bit her lip, tears welling in her eyes. "In case you hadn't noticed, I don't really get along with many people. They were all Dane's friends at Feeney's. One guess as to whose side they will be on."

Jessie searched her face, knowing he couldn't say no to her, not when she was so vulnerable. He had never seen this side of her before. She'd always seemed so confident, so aloof. Turning her down would only make them both feel worse.

He brushed a finger under her eye, catching the tears before they fell.

"You can stay. I can't have you being homeless now, can I?" He smiled. "Go and grab your things. Just don't take too long. I don't want to upset Dane any more than we have already."

"Thanks, babe. It'll just be a few days, I promise." She stood on tippy toes to plant a soft kiss on his lips before jogging to the bedroom to pack her few belongings.

Jessie went to the window, watching for any signs of Dane's return. The last thing he would want to see when he came back home, was Jessie escorting his ex-girlfriend to his place. He knew it was a big mistake to let her stay, but what else could he do? When Sacha had said she didn't have anyone to turn to, there had been so much pain in her eyes. She may act like a tough, sassy woman, but deep down, he could see she was really just a scared girl who was desperate for acceptance. Somehow, that made her more alluring. He felt the undeniable need to protect her, and he would.

Now, if only he could keep his friendship with Dane intact too. That would be the real challenge.

Chapter 14

Maddi had been working for Rachel for a week when she asked her to go out for coffee. Recently single herself, Rachel had noticed that Maddi seemed a little distracted.

"Is everything okay, hon?" Rachel asked as they walked to their table.

"Yeah, everything's fine." Maddi smiled, pulling her seat out.

"Are you sure? You seem preoccupied."

"Oh sorry." She sighed. "I've just been thinking a lot. I'm a bit confused."

"About what?"

"Well, there's this guy."

"Of course there is. It's always a guy." Rachel smiled.

"Yeah," Maddi agreed. "He just seems to have disappeared off the face of the earth."

"What do you mean?"

Maddi stirred the foam around her cup before answering. "One minute we were having a good time, dancing and hanging out, the next minute, he vanishes. I haven't seen or heard from him."

"That's odd. Who's the guy?"

"Jessie. We were in beginners' together. I thought we had a connection."

Rachel pursed her lips.

"You know something, don't you?" Maddi leaned forward.

"I do." She nodded, frowning.

The penny dropped. "Oh… It's Sacha, isn't it?"

"I'm afraid so. I didn't realise you and Jessie were…"

"Oh no! We weren't. But I thought maybe we might. He seemed pretty keen. At least, I thought he was. I obviously read that one wrong." Maddi shrugged. "Well, at least now I know. I just wish he could've told me. Why would he just avoid me?"

"Your guess is as good as mine." Rachel took a sip from her coffee. "You know what? I have something that'll make you feel better."

"What's that?"

"A party! One of the guys is throwing one tonight. You wanna go?"

"I don't know."

"Come on, it'll be fun! We can let our hair down and forget about boys. What do you say?"

Maddi couldn't help but grin back at her new friend. A party did sound like fun.

"Sure. Why not?"

"Great! I'll let them know we're coming."

Dane had spent the days after walking in on Sacha and Jessie in a daze. He had never thought either one was capable of hurting him so much. How wrong he had been.

To make matters worse, he was pretty sure they were actually living together. Sacha had never really had any girlfriends to call on, and when he saw all her things were gone, he just knew that's where she'd be.

After a week of seeking solace in the bottom of a bottle, Dane had decided he needed to do something with friends to get out of his funk. A problem shared is a problem halved, or so they say. He had sent a bulk text out to all his dancer friends, inviting them to his place for a party.

He was several drinks in when he noticed a familiar face walking through the door. She was tall and slender, with bouncing golden curls. He couldn't quite put his finger on where he knew her from, but he knew he had definitely seen her before. You don't forget a face like that.

He watched as she quietly followed Rachel around the room being introduced to the others. She looked out of her depth, and he couldn't really blame her. It would be more than a little intimidating, walking into a room filled with half-drunk people that you had never met before.

Deciding to take matters into his own hands, he approached her.

"What are ya drinking?" he asked, plastering a grin across his face.

"Oh, ah, I brought a bottle of wine. I just need a glass if you have one, please," Maddi said, holding up her drink.

"One glass, coming up!" he said, pulling open a cupboard. "I'm Dane, by the way. I'm not sure if we've met before. You seem familiar, but that could be the booze talking." He chuckled.

"Oh, *you're* Dane," she exclaimed nervously. She hadn't expected to meet him here. "Um, it's nice to meet you. I'm Maddison." She held her hand out to shake, but Dane just grinned.

"You're with dancers—we're huggers here," he said, pulling her in for a big bear hug.

"Oh!" she said again, letting herself be pulled into his embrace.

"You'll have to get used to that, we all do it." He smiled, waving his arms to include the entire room. "Let me help you with that." He took the bottle from her hands and expertly removed the cork. "You've got some catching up to do. I've been mixing up cocktails for everyone all night. You have to try one. It's kinda compulsory." He winked.

"Sure." Maddi smiled, sipping her wine, already feeling more at ease.

"I see you've met Dane," Rachel said as she joined them. "This girl is one of our up-and-coming dancers. Definitely one to watch." She beamed, throwing an arm around Maddi's shoulders. "She's even joined the ladies troupe."

"That so?" Dane asked, his interest piqued. "As it happens, I'm in the running for a new dance partner. I'll have to give you a spin later."

"I'm just a beginner. I bet there's other girls who would love to partner you."

"Did I just get shut down? I'm crushed." Dane pretended to stab a stake through his heart.

"I didn't mean it that way!" Maddi laughed. "I just… I've heard how good you are. I'm not really up to your standard."

"I'll be the judge of that." He smiled, holding his hand out to her. "Come on, let's see what you can do."

Maddi looked at Rachel, who just smiled and pushed her forward. She took his hand and followed him to a clear spot on the lounge floor. He grabbed the iPod and flicked to one of his favourite salsa tracks.

"This is a good one," he said, tapping his feet. He tugged on her arm until she stepped forward enough for him to slide his other arm around to her back. Smiling down at her, he began to move his feet in the basic step. "I have had a few, so excuse my lead."

"I think I can forgive you." Maddi grinned, happy to be dancing. She was most at ease when moving her body to music.

Dane led her through several basic combos before throwing a few together at once. To his pleasure, Maddi followed perfectly.

"You know, I think Rachel might be right. You *are* good."

"Thanks, but forgive me if I don't believe you until you've danced with me sober," she joked. "You may find you have a completely different opinion then.”

“I doubt that. I know a good dancer when I see one.”

Maddi looked at her feet as she felt her face redden.

“Not good at taking compliments, huh?” Dane chuckled. “That’s something else you’d better get used to. You’re one of us now.” He spun her across the floor, into the arms of one of the other men.

“Oh!” She giggled as he continued the dance before spinning her back to Dane. “That was fun!”

“It’s a little trick we like to call ‘hi-jacking’.” He lowered her into a dip to finish the song. “I think it’s time for another drink, don’t you?”

“Sure,” Maddi said breathlessly. She skipped back to the kitchen to retrieve her wine. Dane busied himself with cocktail mixing.

“You look like you’re having a good time,” Rachel said, a glint in her eye.

“Yeah, I am. Thanks for bringing me. It’s just what I needed.

“What do you think of Dane?”

“He’s great fun to dance with.” She beamed.

“Well, yeah of course. But I mean, what do you *think* of him?”

“What?” Maddi frowned before her eyes lit up and she covered her mouth with her hand. “Oh! No, he’s not really my type. He seems really nice though.”

“Oh, that’s a shame.” Rachel pouted.

"Get these into ya, ladies." Dane appeared with two tall glasses filled with an amber liquid. "It's got vanilla Galliano, vodka, peach schnapps and orange juice in it."

"Mmm, that's delicious!" Rachel said.

Maddi nodded in agreeance. "Yeah, it really is. Are you a bartender?"

Dane laughed. "I wish. Nah, I just like to experiment." He raised his glass to the two of them. "To new friends." They each clinked their glasses together.

"To new friends!" they chimed back, laughing.

Chapter 15

Several drinks and dances later, Dane finally remembered where he had seen Maddi before.

"Snickers!" he bellowed with a grin.

"Excuse me?" Maddi asked, nearly choking on her drink.

"That's where I know you from! You were the girl who couldn't decide which chocolate bar to buy." He chuckled. "I knew I'd remember eventually."

"That was you? That's a little embarrassing."

"Why? Because you thought I was a stalker?" he joked. Maddi couldn't help but giggle.

"All I could hear were these heavy footsteps getting closer and a man yelling out to me. Can you blame me?" She laughed.

"Heavy footsteps? What am I? An elephant?" Dane put on an unconvincing hurt expression.

"You know what I mean!" She giggled again.

"I might have to teach you a lesson for that." He leaped up and scooped her into his arms, making her squeal.

"Put me down!"

"I can't hear you!" He swung her up and into the air, passing her onto one of the other guys there.

She shrieked as she was thrown from guy-to-guy around the room. This was the most fun she had had in a long time.

Once she was back in Dane's arms, he placed her gently down on the ground with a huge grin on his face. She playfully swatted his arm.

"I can't believe you just did that!" she said, pretending to be cross.

"Didn't you enjoy being thrown around like a rag doll?" he asked, smirking.

She thought about continuing the charade of being upset, but the smile spreading across her face betrayed her. "Actually, it was pretty fun," she admitted. "I can honestly say I've never been thrown around a room before."

"Glad to entertain you." He bowed down before her.

"That looked interesting." Rachel joined them.

"Yeah, you could say that." Maddi chuckled. "Quite exhilarating actually."

"You're very trusting to let a group of drunks throw you about." She laughed. "I would've been afraid they'd drop me."

Maddi's jaw dropped. "I didn't even think about that!" She swatted Dane again.

"Hey! We would never have dropped you!"

"Hmmm." Maddi pursed her lips. "I'll let it slide… this time." She pointed a finger at him. "But only because I'm having so much fun."

"Good to hear it. Must be time for another dance then." He grabbed her hand before she could turn him down, pulling her out to the centre of the room. He leaned in to whisper in her ear. "You know what?" he asked.

"What?"

"I think we make a great team."

"Oh really? What are you basing this on?"

"Well, I helped you with your chocolate buying, we dance well together—even under the influence, *and* I can throw you around without dropping you." He winked. Maddi laughed.

"That makes us a good team?"

"Yep. Think about it. If we can dance this fantastically while drinking, we will be even more amazing when we're sober," he said matter-of-factly.

"I have to admit, that's a pretty good argument. I see a flaw though."

"What's that?"

She leaned in. "Maybe we just *think* we're dancing fantastically, when in actual fact… we suck." She tilted her head, brows raised, waiting for his response.

"I cannot believe you just said I suck at dancing," Dane said in mock outrage.

"Wait, that's not what I said. I said *we* suck." She pointed her finger between the two of them. "Us together. Under the influence. Not you by yourself. You're great!" She rushed the words, trying not to offend him.

"So, you admit it then?"

"Admit what?"

"That I'm great." He smirked.

"You, are just twisting my words!" She laughed. As much as he wasn't her type, she was having a great time hanging out. He had a magnetic quality to him.

If she was completely honest with herself, she agreed—she did think they made a good team. She just hoped that he would still feel the same once he had sobered up. Having Dane as a dance partner would be a lot of fun. Having someone to practise with regularly would be good for her dancing too. Not to mention the added bonus of getting back at Sacha for the way she had spoken to her, and maybe for taking Jessie from her. Not that he was 'hers' to be taken in the first place. But she did feel as though she had lost a friend.

"What's going through your mind right now?" Dane asked, poking her nose. "You look all serious all of a sudden."

"Nothing important." She smiled. "Must be time for a top-up." She wiggled her glass in the air.

"Your wish is my command." He took her glass back to the kitchen to mix up yet another cocktail.

Maddi pushed thoughts of Sacha and Jessie to the back of her mind. Tonight was about feeling good and forgetting the bad. She stood on legs that were more jelly than she had anticipated and wobbled her way into the kitchen.

"How strong are you pouring these?" she asked, leaning against the bench for stability. "If I didn't know better, I'd think you were trying to get me drunk." She grinned.

"Ah curses! She's onto me!" He winked, handing her another drink.

"Wait, I can't tell if you're serious or not," she said, confused.

"Relax, Maddi. I'm not gonna jump you. I prefer my women to be of sound mind." He grinned.

"I don't know if I should be offended by that or not!" She laughed. "But I'm going to choose to believe you mean you wouldn't take advantage of a drunk." She swirled her straw around her glass before taking a sip. "Ooh that's good! This is definitely my favourite," she said.

"I bet you say that to all the boys."

Chapter 16

Maddi stumbled back home in the early hours of the morning. She tried hard to conceal her giggles as she knocked the coat rack—and by some miracle—managed to catch it before it crashed to the floor. She did, however, smack it into the wall and drop half the coats. Shushing herself, she stooped down to pick them back up, bracing herself against the door frame.

"Having fun?" Rory asked, tying her robe as she padded out of her room.

"Oh-my-gosh! Sssorry! I dint meanto wake you," Maddi slurred, a drunken grin plastered across her face. "I might've hadda bit-too muchta drink." She giggled, collapsing in a heap on the coats.

"Come here, you big dork. Let me help you up." Rory smiled, happy to see her friend had had a good night.

"Bending is hard." Maddi frowned before erupting into yet another fit of laughter. Rory grabbed her hands and pulled. Maddi folded in half, which made her laugh even more.

"You have to help too! Plant your feet!" Rory laughed.

"Okay, sssorry. I'mma try this time." Maddi put on a serious face, pulling her knees in. She managed to get to her feet this time, and with the help of Rory, she made it to her room. She plonked down on the edge of her bed, flopping backwards. "Bed is good."

"Yes, it is. Are you going to be alright? You need a bucket?"

"Huh?" Maddi said, her eyes already beginning to close.

Rory pulled her shoes off and rolled her under the covers as best she could. She went to the kitchen and poured her a glass of water to leave on her nightstand. Smiling, she switched the light off before heading back to her own room.

The next morning, Rory was busy in the kitchen when a squinty-eyed Maddi made her way out to join her.

"What time is it?" she croaked.

"Eleven."

"You should've woken me!"

"Why? You got big plans today? You got in pretty late last night, I figured you could do with the sleep." Rory grinned.

"Oh God, did I wake you?"

"Well, you were dancing with the coat rack outside my bedroom door, so it was a little hard to ignore," she teased. Maddi held her head in her hands. "Bit of a headache?"

"Mmm. Just a bit. Do we have any juice?"

"As a matter of fact, we do." She poured a large glass and handed it to her. Maddi gulped it back. "Woah, tiger Not too fast. I am *not* cleaning up spew. That's where I draw the line."

"Sorry, I'm just so thirsty."

"Yeah, that'll happen when you've been up all night, drinking." She helped herself to a glass of juice too. "Now, I know you're a lightweight, but one bottle of wine is not enough to get you off your face like that. So, who was supplying you with all the booze? A guy, perhaps?" She raised her brows with a knowing grin.

"Yeah, actually. You won't believe who it was," Maddi said, remembering the many cocktails she had consumed last night as her stomach began to gurgle. "Oh, that's not good." She held her hand to her middle, as if trying to keep the contents of her stomach from escaping.

"Don't you dare!" Rory pointed a finger. Maddi swallowed a few times, taking deep breaths.

"I think I'm okay," she said quietly.

"You sure?"

"Yip." Maddi nodded. "I might go have a shower."

"Good idea, I didn't wanna say anything before…" Rory joked, poking her tongue out at her friend.

"If I could, I'd throw something at you right now. You're lucky I'm hungover." She attempted to scowl, but her mouth betrayed her, lifting at the corners.

She dragged herself to the bathroom. The lights were too bright for her eyes, so she turned them off and left the door ajar, letting the glow of the hall light streak through. She turned the shower on and peeled her clothes off, leaving them in a heap on the floor. She stepped under the hot water, letting it cascade down her back, washing away the night before.

When she got out, she wrapped herself in a big fluffy towel and felt almost human again. She saw that Rory had left some clothes for her on the floor by the door. Her big comfy trackies, a singlet, and her favourite hoody. Definitely hangover clothes if ever there was.

A coffee and slice of cake were waiting for her when she finally emerged from the bathroom.

"You look better," Rory said, leaning on the counter, sipping from her own cup.

"Thanks, I feel it." Maddi smiled, grabbing her goodies and folding herself up on the couch.

"So, before you cleaned yourself up, you were about to tell me about the guy you were with last night." Rory followed her to the couch. "Spill." She sat facing Maddi in eager anticipation.

"Don't go getting all excited, it's nothing like that!" Maddi laughed. "We just hung out."

"Oh, that's no fun." She pouted. "You made it sound all exciting. Are you sure you didn't just misread the signs?"

"Okay, I don't know about him, but *I'm* not interested in him like that."

"What would you know? You were drunk!" Rory tried again. "The state you were in last night, I'm surprised you could even remember your own name."

"I wasn't that bad. Was I?"

"I've seen worse. But if this guy was pouring drinks down your throat, he's either keen or a creep."

"I don't think he's a creep. I didn't get that vibe off him." She scrunched her nose. "I haven't even told you who it was yet. You'll never believe it."

"Well?"

"You remember super-bitch, Sacha?"

"Yeah, of course. She wasn't there, was she? Ooh! Did you knock her out?!"

"Yeah, totally. That's what I did." Maddi snorted. "Of course I didn't! And no, she wasn't there. But Dane was."

"No way! You hooked up with her boyfriend? Gold!" Rory hooted, practically dancing in her seat.

"Firstly, he's not her boyfriend anymore, and secondly, I didn't hook up with him. But he *was* the one pouring the drinks. We hung out all night. He said we make a good team." She smiled. "If he remembers, I think he may ask me to be his dance partner."

"Not quite as good as hooking up with him, but it's a start. But rewind a bit there. They're not together anymore?" she asked.

"Nope. Turns out, she *is* Jessie's type."

"You're kidding?!" Rory gaped. "I did *not* see that coming."

"It explains why we haven't seen him lately."

"I guess. Pretty rude though, if you ask me."

"You don't know the half of it. Rachel told me Dane walked in on them… ya know… gettin' busy."

"Eww gross!" Rory stuck her tongue out, making retching sounds.

"I know. Poor Dane though. That's pretty rough."

"I reckon. More reason for you two to work together then. Show them up on the dancefloor. I bet Sacha couldn't stand to have someone else in the lime-light."

"You could be onto something there. It would be nice to take her down a peg or two," Maddi agreed. "I'm gonna have to start practising if I'm going to show her up though."

Chapter 17

"So, I was thinking…" Sacha drawled as she lay across Jessie's stomach.

"Mmm?" he said, stroking her hair.

"How would you feel about entering the salsa comps with me?" She looked up, her eyes full of hope.

"You're joking, right?"

"Nope. I'm one hundred percent serious."

"I've only just started dancing. I'm not ready to compete!"

Sacha sat up, folding her legs beneath her. "Sure you are. You're picking it up really fast, and the comps are still a few months away; we've got plenty of time to whip you into shape." She grinned.

"I dunno…"

"Please?" she begged, holding her hands as if in prayer. "Pretty please. I really wanna enter with you." Pausing for effect, she added, "I'll do anything you want me to," in a sing-song voice.

Jessie laughed. "Okay, okay. If that's what you really want, I'll do it."

"Yay! Thank you, thank you, thank you!" she squealed, leaning over to kiss him. "We are gonna kick arse!" She clapped her hands together excitedly. "I've already got a heap of ideas."

"How about we get me confident with the basics first, and then we can start planning for the comps." Jessie smiled.

"Oh, alright then, spoil sport." Sacha pouted. Jessie ran a finger around her lips.

"I believe there was a promise to do anything I wanted." He waggled his brows suggestively.

"Promise? I don't recall making any such promises," Sacha said, full of innocence. Jessie lunged, pulling her down on top of him once more. She giggled in delight. "Okay! What do you want?" she asked.

"I'm sure we can come up with some sort of arrangement," he said, running his hand through her hair and kissing her.

"I like your way of thinking," Sacha said breathlessly. Jessie rolled so that Sacha was pinned beneath him. She wrapped her legs around his waist, pulling him closer to her. He held her hands and drew them up behind her head. Holding them in one hand, he used his other to trace down her arm, making her squirm. He continued down her side, until his hand was cupping her behind. Lowering his head, he kissed from her shoulder, up her neck and back to her lips.

Sacha wiggled her hips against him as she hungrily kissed him back. She wanted to touch him, but he had her hands firmly in his grasp.

"Let me touch you," she breathed. Jessie grinned against her lips.

"Oh, but this is much too fun."

"Tease," she said hoarsely.

"Oh, you think so, do you?" He kissed a trail down her neck, lifting her top to expose her creamy skin. He flicked his tongue across her stomach, slowly making his way to the waistband of her jeans. Sacha watched him with eager eyes. She lifted her hips as he skilfully removed her pants with one hand.

He ran his hand up her leg as he lightly kissed his way up her inner thigh. Sacha moaned, arching her back and drawing her knees up. Jessie paused with a wicked grin on his face.

"*Now*, you can call me a tease," he said, getting up off the bed. Sacha stared at him, mouth gaping open.

"You did *not* just do that!" she said, throwing a cushion at him. Jessie laughed.

"Hey, you called it."

"Well, now I'm un-calling it. Get over here and finish what you started!" she demanded, kneeling on the bed. She slowly peeled her top over her head as he watched.

"Seeing as you asked so nicely…" he murmured, unable to tear his eyes away as she ran her hands over her body enticingly. With one step he was tangled in her arms once more.

"That was amazing," Jessie stated, running a finger up and down Sacha's arm as she cuddled into his side.

"I know." She grinned, kissing his chest.

"Still so modest." Jessie chuckled.

"Hey, you don't get to be this fantastic without blowing your own trumpet. No-one else is gonna do it for you," she said matter-of-factly.

"That's a bit of a morbid way of looking at things, don't ya think?"

"Just saying it how it is."

Jessie pulled her in tightly, kissing the top of her head. Sacha certainly was a different breed of woman. He had never met someone so brutally honest before. There was more to her than met the eye.

"Come on, if we're gonna "kick arse" at these comps, we'd better get practising. I've got a long way to go," Jessie said, throwing the crumpled sheets off and swinging his legs over the edge of the bed. Sacha snaked her arm around his waist.

"That's why we're so good together. We're both driven." She kissed his back. "Now go get cleaned up!" She swatted his behind teasingly. "We've got a lot of work to do."

"Yes, drill sergeant!" He saluted her before marching to the shower.

Sacha stretched out on the bed, pleased with herself. She had chosen well this time. Not only was he amazing in bed, he was also ambitious and competitive—qualities she held in high regard.

His desire to be nice to everyone was his one flaw, though she had every intention of using it to her advantage. There was no way she was going to look for another place to stay, and she knew Jessie would never kick her out. She had him right where she wanted him.

Now, to keep him from learning her secret plan for the comps. What she had up her sleeve was sure to win them first place. She just had to keep him away from Dane.

Chapter 18

"Are you sure this isn't a date?" Rory asked sceptically.

"Positive. Now get ready!" Maddi replied, shoving her towards the door. "He'll be here soon."

"I don't wanna be the third wheel," she whined.

"You won't be. Go!" Maddi pointed across the hall. Rory padded back to her room to change.

Much to Maddi's delight, Dane had invited them to go to Feeney's with him this week. She hadn't seen him since the party and was looking forward to dancing with him again. Dancing with the beginners in class just didn't cut it after being flung around the room by a pro.

Stepping back and inspecting herself in the mirror, Maddi was satisfied. She brushed on a little lip gloss before sauntering into Rory's room to see if she was ready.

"How do I look?" Rory twirled, fishnet-gloved hands on hips. "Do I pass?"

"Sure do. You look great!" Maddi clapped her hands. It never ceased to amaze her how quickly her friend could get ready to go out. She was dressed in an off-the-shoulder crop-top with cut-off denim shorts. Her short blonde hair was spiked up in all directions and she had attached a thin headband over top. High-top sneakers with a built-in heel finished off her look. She could be quite the fashionista when she wanted to be.

Maddi, on the other hand, went for a sleeker look. Black leggings with diamantes down the sides, coupled with a deep purple singlet and matching heels. She wore a silver tasselled scarf around her hips. Her hair was half tied up, the rest curling around her face and down her back.

"You look pretty good yourself." Rory grinned, giving her the once over.

There was a knock at the door. Maddi and Rory quickly grabbed their bags and both went to answer it.

"Hey." Dane waved. "You two look stunning."

"Thanks." Maddi smiled warmly before gesturing to her friend. "This is my flatmate, Rory."

"Nice to meet you, Rory." Dane offered his hand.

"Likewise," she said, shaking his hand firmly. "I hear you're quite the dancer."

"That so?" Dane raised his brow at Maddi with a sly grin. "What else has she been saying about me?"

"Only that you plastered her with alcohol at the party the other night." Rory held her hand up for a high five. "Well done you."

Dane chuckled and slapped his hand against hers.

"Shall we get our dance on then?" she asked.

"Absolutely. Do you dance salsa too?"

"Me? Not really. I've been to a few classes, but that's about it."

"We'll have to change that then." He winked, ushering them out the door.

They kept up a steady banter on their way into town. Dane was a pretty smooth talker; it was clear to see why he was so popular.

"Have you guys been to Feeney's before?" he asked.

"Actually, my dance troupe performed here last week. It was pretty fun," Maddi said.

"Oh, that's right." A flicker of something crossed his face before he schooled his expression. "I'm sorry I missed it." He smiled, changing the subject. "They play the best music here, don't they?"

"Yeah. It's nice to hear new songs. I didn't realise there were so many different styles." Maddi smiled at the memory.

"Stick with me, kid, I'll show you them all! And I promise, you won't get thrown around this time." He grinned mischievously.

Maddi giggled. "I should hope not! That was a one-time-only thing."

"Okay, I'm confused. Is this some dance lingo I don't understand?" Rory frowned.

"Didn't I tell you about that?" Maddi laughed.

"Clearly not." She rolled her eyes.

"I may have picked Maddi up and thrown her around the room last weekend. Kinda like pass-the-parcel," Dane explained, "only it was pass-Maddi."

"Wait, you *literally* threw her around the room? That's kinda badarse." Rory rounded on Maddi. "I can't believe you missed that part out of the story!"

"It *was* pretty fun," Maddi admitted. Dane opened his mouth to speak, but Maddi jumped in first. "But never again!" She pointed her finger at his chest.

"Oh alright then," he huffed. "Come on, we're here," he said grabbing their hands and leading them through the doors. "You guys want a drink?"

"Sure," they chimed together.

"What'll you have?"

"Surprise us," Rory said, dragging Maddi to a table. They draped their bags over the back of a chair and sat down. "He seems pretty cool."

"Yeah. Wait until you see him dance," Maddi said. "He's amazing." She scanned the room to see if anyone from class was there. "Oh my God!" she half squealed, turning to face Rory with her mouth gaping open. "Look who just walked in," she hissed, pointing behind her.

"Is that Jessie?"

"And Sacha," Maddi whispered.

"*That's* Sacha? Wow. Not what I had pictured at all," Rory said, surprised. "She's so tiny. You could take her, easy." She narrowed her eyes with a nod of her head.

"Something tells me she would fight dirty." Maddi scowled. "Is it wrong that she irritates me this much?"

"Are you kidding? I haven't even met her and I'm irritated," Rory scoffed.

"Here's your drinks. Vodka and Red Bull. Hope you like it." Dane grinned as he placed their drinks in front of them.

"Ooh, sounds tasty," Rory said taking a big swig. "Mmm, it is. I think this will be my new favourite drink." She raised her glass to Dane.

"You okay, Maddi? You look like you've seen a ghost," Dane asked.

"Uh yeah, I'm fine." She glanced behind her with a wince. "I'm just not sure how happy you're going to be."

"Why's that?" He followed her line of sight. "Oh... I see." His smile faded momentarily. "No big deal. There's room here for all of us, right?" He chugged his drink back. "I just might go get another one of these." He stood and made his way back to the bar with slumped shoulders.

"Poor guy," Rory said quietly.

"Yeah. I feel so bad for him. Maybe we should leave."

"No! You can't let her see that she's having any kind of effect. Just pretend like she isn't even here."

"Easier said than done," she said, plastering a smile on her face as Dane approached. "Hey, you wanna hit the dancefloor?"

"Sure." He smiled back with a look of relief. He clasped her hand in his and led her to the middle of the dancefloor.

"Go easy on me." She grinned.

"Not a chance." He winked, sweeping her into a low dip. He spun her around the floor for several dances, the tension easing with each one. Maddi was pleased that she was still able to keep up with him.

"Um, wow! That was amazing! You two look so good together!" Rory whistled when they finally joined her at the table again. "I didn't know you could do all those moves!" She nudged her friend with her elbow.

"I didn't either." Maddi laughed. "He's a good teacher."

"Why, thank you. You're a really light lead, it's a nice change." He looked at Maddi with a goofy grin.

"I see you've found a new toy already, Dane. It seems we're not that different after all," Sacha said condescendingly as she came up behind him.

Dane stood to face her. "Sacha," he said. "Decided to crawl out from under your rock I see." He took a mouthful of his drink. "Have you met Maddi? My *new* dance partner?" He placed his hand on the small of her back.

Without missing a beat, Maddi held her hand out.

"Hi," she said sweet as pie. Sacha eyeballed her hand as if it were covered in mud.

"We've met," she said with disgust.

"This is Jessie. We *used* to be friends," Dane said, motioning to Jessie. He couldn't bear to look him in the eye. "Oh, that's right. You two know each other already, don't you?" He waved his drink between them.

"We do," Maddi agreed. "It's good to see you're still alive, Jessie," she said coolly.

"I deserve that. Sorry." He shifted uncomfortably. "I... I never meant to..."

"Yeah, we've heard that before," Dane interrupted, his eyes wandering around the room in boredom. Jessie looked back at Maddi.

"You look really nice," he said with a small smile. Sacha shot him a dirty look.

"Well, Jessie is *my* new dance partner," she said, drawing the attention away from Maddi. "We're going to compete this year."

"That so?" Dane asked. "Well, isn't that a coincidence? So are we," he announced, glancing sideways at Maddi.

"You two?" Sacha scoffed. "Good luck with that." She laughed mockingly, looking Maddi up and down.

Determined not to let her get to her, Maddi simply said, "Same to you."

"May the best man win then," Jessie said, offering his hand to Dane with a smile.

"Is that meant to be some kind of joke?"

"No, I… I didn't mean it like that, man," Jessie stammered, dropping his hand to his side. "Forget I said anything."

"Don't worry, I plan to," Dane spat.

"Come on, babe," Sacha said, looking up at Jessie. "Let's go have a dance. I'm tired of this now." She grabbed his hand and dragged him to the dancefloor. Jessie gave Maddi an apologetic look before turning away.

"Well, that sure was fun," Rory commented from behind them.

"You can say that again." Maddi slumped down in her seat.

"Sorry, I kinda threw you in it back there. I totally understand if you don't wanna be my dance partner. I just couldn't let her have something else over me," Dane said.

"It's fine. I'd love to be your dance partner." Maddi's face reddened as she added, "I was kinda hoping you would ask."

"Really? Great!" He beamed. "And the comps too?" he asked with hope.

"Sure. Why not? May as well go the whole hog." She shrugged. She knew it was childish, but she really wanted to wipe that smug smile off Sacha's face. Beating her at the comps would hit her where it hurt the most—her ego.

Chapter 19

"Can you believe those two?" Rory asked, disgusted. "Get a room!" she yelled across the crowded floor.

Sacha had straddled Jessie's lap and was giving him an impromptu lap dance. To his credit, Jessie appeared embarrassed by the display and kept trying to get her to stop. Sacha clearly had other ideas though.

"How can she be such a bitch? This must be killing Dane," Maddi said with a sigh. She glanced over at the bar, hoping he hadn't noticed the little show Sacha was putting on. He had.

He stood with his drink in hand, watching with a look of pure hatred in his eyes. His fingers were taught around the glass he was holding, the knuckles white from the pressure. If he wasn't careful, it'd shatter.

Maddi waved out, and reluctantly, it seemed, he tore his eyes away from the scene before him. Tipping his glass back, he slammed it on the bar and made his way over.

"You okay?" Maddi asked gently. She reached out and put her hand over his.

"Yeah, I'm fine," he grimaced. It was obvious he was trying to hold his composure, but it was getting harder to keep his cool. And rightly so. Dane had every right to be mad. He had not said one wrong word against them even though they had hurt him deeply with their betrayal. Now he was having to endure it in public too. How could they be so cruel?

"We can go if you want. I don't mind," Maddi offered.

"No, it's fine," he said through his teeth. "Let's just have a dance."

"Whatever you need." She allowed herself to be led to the centre of the dancefloor. It was a bachata playing. Maddi recognised the beat but hadn't actually tried it before. "I'm not sure how the steps go," she admitted.

"That's okay. Just listen to the music and let it flow through you. You'll pick it up easily. We don't have to do anything fancy." He smiled, pulling her in close. "Wrap your hands around my neck. Just follow my lead."

They began swaying to the music. Maddi closed her eyes, letting it flood over her. It had such a beautiful melody that she found herself getting caught up in it. Dane leaned forward, leading her through a slow, circular dip. He held her against his body and slowly went through the steps with her. As predicted, she followed without too many hiccups.

"That felt wonderful," she said dreamily. "The music just begs to be danced to."

Dane smiled. "It's my favourite style of dance."

"I can see why."

They went back to the table, and this time, Dane pulled Rory up for a salsa.

"Wish me luck!" she called back.

"Luck!" Maddi laughed. She took a quick mouthful of her drink before heading to the bathroom to freshen up. It was pretty hot out on the floor.

She splashed some water on her face and was dabbing it dry with a paper towel when the door swung open and in sauntered Sacha.

"What do you think you're playing at?" she demanded, coming up behind Maddi.

"Excuse me?" Maddi turned to face her.

"Don't act dumb. Swooping in, taking my sloppy seconds. You think you actually have a shot at the comps?" She smirked, folding her arms across her chest and jutting her hip out.

Maddi squared her shoulders. "Yeah. I do."

"He's going nowhere. Jessie is where it's at. We *will* win," she spat.

"Who're you trying to convince? Me or you?" Maddi asked, smiling.

"Sweetheart, I can out-dance you with my eyes closed," Sacha snarled, leaning in close. "You haven't got a hope in hell." She turned on her heel and stalked out.

Maddi shook her head in disbelief. How can she be so vicious to someone she barely knows? It was mind-boggling. But it set things in place in Maddi's mind. She was going to show Sacha.

She left the bathroom and joined Dane and Rory at the table.

"We are going to have to start training. There is no way I'm letting her beat us," she said.

"Did she jump you in the bathroom?" Rory asked, leaping to her feet, ready for a fight. Maddi calmly gestured for her to take a seat.

"Not quite. She *did* come and tell me she was better than me," Maddi said.

"Right. That's it." Dane stood and marched over to Sacha, tapping her on the shoulder. "You can't bear the fact that I found a better dancer than you, can you?" he demanded.

"Who? *Her*?" Sacha pointed at Maddi. "Don't make me laugh!" she scoffed.

"Look, I've held my tongue so far, but not anymore. You're so sure you can beat us? Put your money where your mouth is," Dane said.

"Alright then. If we win," she pointed a finger to his chest, "you have to find another dance partner." She raised her brows with a wicked grin.

Dane barely batted an eye. "Deal. And *when* we win—and we *will* win—you two," he pointed between her and Jessie, "have to stay away from Feeney's."

"Deal." They shook hands. "Good luck finding another partner!" Sacha called out as he walked away. He didn't bother biting back.

"What was that all about?" Maddi asked when he sat back down.

"We *have* to beat her," Dane said.

"Okay."

"No, we *really* have to beat her. Otherwise," he paused, looking sheepish, "I have to find another dance partner."

"Oh."

"You didn't seriously bet on it, did you?" Rory asked.

"Don't worry. We got this. One thing I know about Sacha—she's no good at choreography. That was always my job." He grinned.

"So, what do *you* get if we win?"

"Those two are not to step foot in Feeney's again." He took a sip of his drink.

"You didn't wanna try and split them up too?" Rory questioned.

"Nah. They can have each other as far as I'm concerned. I'm done with them."

Chapter 20

The next day, Dane showed up on Maddi's doorstep with three takeaway coffees and a bag of croissants.

"I brought breakfast." He grinned goofily. "Thought if you didn't have any plans, we could get straight into training."

"You certainly are determined." Maddi smiled, taking one of the warm cups from him and inhaling. "Mmm, coffee." She sighed, taking a gulp. "Rory! Dane brought coffee!" she called over her shoulder. She stepped aside, ushering Dane into their home.

"Did someone say coffee?" Rory mumbled as she shuffled out of her room, bleary eyed and dishevelled.

"Uh-huh. And croissants." Maddi held the bag and cup out enticingly.

"Gimme." Rory reached for them. "Oh, sweet coffee, how I love thee." She settled on the couch, her hands wrapped around the warm cup. "To what do we owe the pleasure?" she asked.

"Sorry, I came too early, didn't I?" Dane said apologetically. "I just wanted to get a jump on the training."

"Geez you're eager."

"I think it's a great idea." Maddi beamed. "I'm going to need a lot of work to get up to Sacha's standard."

Dane frowned. "You need to stop doing that."

"What?"

"Putting yourself down. You're just as good as she is."

"Hardly!" Maddi scoffed. "She's been doing this style a lot longer than I have."

"So? It's obvious you've danced before."

"Well, yeah, but it's not the same, is it?"

"No, it's not. It's better." He winked. "Sacha's all about the attention. Believe me, if she didn't think you were a threat, she wouldn't be getting this worked up about it."

"Listen to the man, he has a point," Rory agreed. Maddi rolled her eyes.

"Trust you to take his side." She finished her coffee and grabbed a croissant from the bag, peeling a chunk off and popping it into her mouth. "I guess I should go change so we can get started," she said around her mouthful, bounding back down the hall.

Sweeping her hair up into a ponytail, she rummaged through her drawer for something comfortable to wear. She settled on a pair of grey yoga pants and a baby pink singlet. After pulling on a pair of ankle tights, she grabbed her old jazz shoes down from the wardrobe shelf. They would do for training, but she was going to have to invest in some proper dance heels now that it had gotten so serious.

Serious was an understatement. The National Salsa Competition was a big deal. Add their wager into the mix, and it's even more so.

"Okay, I'm ready," she said as she breezed back into the lounge. "Where shall we start?"

"Okay, well, I thought maybe we could use this song." He pushed play on his iPod, and a beautiful guitar solo filled the room. "We could start off with a shine, and when the beat comes in, go into some combos. How are you with lifts?" His eyes shone with an excitement Maddi had never seen before.

"Ah, good, I guess. I've never really done them before, but I've always wanted to try."

"Great. We can try a few out, see what feels comfortable, and then incorporate those into the choreography. What do you think of the song?"

"It's beautiful."

"Yeah, it is," Dane said with a smile. "You wanna see what I have planned so far?"

"You've already got moves worked out?" She shook her head with a laugh. "That's impressive."

"Yeah, well…" Dane shrugged his shoulders. "I couldn't sleep last night," he admitted. "After we decided on entering, I just had all these ideas floating around in my head. Couldn't shut my brain off until I got up and started working through some steps."

"The curse of an artist," Maddi said. "Better show me what you've got then."

Dane handed his iPod to Rory and got into position. She hit play once again and he began moving his feet to the strum of the guitar. He danced with such grace, almost as if he were floating on air. His fancy footwork was flawless, his spins sharp. Maddi could hardly believe he had only just come up with this stuff.

Rory whistled from her perch on the couch. "The guy sure can move."

"He certainly can. Dane, that was amazing!" Maddi beamed as she pulled her ponytail tighter. "Can you break it down for me?"

"Of course. You really like it?"

"I really do." She put her hand on his arm. "It's fantastic."

"Thanks." He smiled, running his hand through his hair. "Okay so we'll have to come up with a starting pose, but basically, it starts like this." He popped his chest back and forth before crossing his feet one in front of the other with a twist. "This is called a Suzy-Q step. You wanna make sure you are twisting your hips to do it, rather than taking big steps. Like this." He demonstrated again. This time, Maddi did it alongside him. "Good."

They continued popping, stepping, and spinning until they were both drenched in sweat. Dane had broken down the entire guitar solo for her, and the more they practiced, the more polished they became.

Rory had filmed them a few times before escaping to her room. They watched it back to see how it looked and what needed work. Other than a few minor changes to make Maddi's moves sleeker and more feminine, they were impressed with their work so far.

"Not bad for our first day of training," Dane said with a smile. "You regretting it yet?"

"Not a chance." Maddi grinned, dabbing her neck with a towel. "That was so much fun. I haven't danced like that in years."

"I find that hard to believe. You're a natural."

A warm glow swept up her neck and cheeks. She wiped the towel across her face to try and hide it. Dane chuckled.

"You're gonna have to face it one of these days. You keep dancing like that and people are going to notice you." He pulled the towel from her hands. "I think you're pretty great, ya know?"

She was suddenly very aware of the fact they were on their own. "I… um. You wanna drink?" she asked, trying to change the subject. His close proximity made her feel a little awkward.

Dane dropped his hands to his side, a small smile on his face. "Sure, a drink would be nice."

"Water? Juice? Coffee?" she asked, walking through to the kitchen, avoiding eye contact. She didn't want him to think they were more than just friends.

"Coffee would be great, thanks," he said. "Milk and two please."

"Sweet. I'll put the jug on. Rory, you want another coffee?" she called down the hall.

"Uh does a cow go moo?"

Maddi sighed quietly in relief. If anyone could diffuse the situation, it was Rory. A long time ago, they had come up with a code for such times as these. After one too many persistent guys who couldn't take a hint, they had devised a plan to help each other out. They had decided on a few different phrases for different situations, so that they would always have an escape if need be.

Maddi locked eyes with Rory when she walked in. "Is that a new top?" she asked, brows raised. Rory frowned, looking over at Dane.

"This old thing?" she asked. "Nope, just haven't worn it in a while. Hey, can you still help me at work today?" She took a seat next to Dane, watching Maddi curiously. "We'll need to leave soon."

They hadn't used the code in years, and she couldn't see why Maddi would need it now. Dane seemed nice enough, he was a good-looking guy, and he could dance, what more could she want?

"Yeah sure, thanks for reminding me, I'd forgotten." Maddi smiled, grateful that her friend had come to her rescue. "Sorry, we'll have to cut the training short," she said apologetically. "Do you mind?"

"No, of course not. I should've checked first anyway." Dane gathered his things together.

"You can stay for that coffee, if you want. I'm sure I have time for a quick drink before I have to get ready." She looked at Rory, who gave a quizzical look.

"Ah, yeah, sure," she muttered, shaking her head. *Talk about mixed messages.*

Chapter 21

Jessie adjusted his stance, ready to try the lift again. They had been at it for an hour, and he still couldn't quite get it mastered.

"Okay, ready?" he asked a flustered Sacha.

"Of course I am!" she snapped. She hadn't anticipated it being so hard to teach a lift. She and Dane had learned together, and it had been a lot easier. Admittedly, they had been watching an instructional DVD—which belonged to Dane. Doing it from memory was proving to be difficult.

"Sorry, I've never done anything like this before. I don't want to hurt you."

"I'm not as fragile as you think. Just throw me over your shoulder like a sack of potatoes."

Jessie laughed at the image. "Okay then, if that's what you want." He bent his knees into a high squat before grabbing her underneath her thigh. Sacha wrapped one arm around his neck and held the other out for balance. "One, two, three!" He did as she asked and flung her like a sack of potatoes until she was perched across his shoulder. "It worked!"

"Easy! Don't wiggle too much or I'll lose my balance!" she said, concentrating on keeping her body straight.

"How do we get out of this?" Jessie asked, realising they hadn't discussed that part yet.

"Grab my hands and lower me down behind you." She slid gracefully down his back. "I knew you could do it!" She grinned, bounding into his arms and planting a kiss on his lips. "You just have to stop treating me like a dainty flower, cos baby, I ain't that soft."

"Yeah, I'm starting to realise that." Jessie chuckled. "You wanna try it again?"

"Sure." She unwrapped her legs from his waist and dropped to the ground. "Better make sure it wasn't just a fluke." She winked, getting herself into position. "Ready when you are."

After another hour, they had perfected both the lift and the dismount. With the comps looming, Sacha was eager to push on through with their routine. There was still a lot to cover before the big day, and she was determined to beat Dane at all costs.

So far, they had about a third of their routine done. Jessie had picked up all the combos with no problems, but the tricks were proving to be hard work.

Now that he had accomplished the main lift though, she felt a slight release of pressure.

There was still so much to do; the other two thirds of the choreography for starters, and then there were costumes to organise, dance shoes to buy. All in a matter of weeks.

Sacha wasn't worried though. Things always worked out for her. It hadn't taken long for Jessie to learn the first part, and she didn't doubt he would pick up the rest without a hitch. The costumes would be easy; if there was one thing she was better at than dancing and seduction, it was shopping. She had visions of a skintight, leaving-nothing-to-the-imagination, dress. She was going to drop jaws.

For Jessie, she had planned on a simple black Latin style suit, with flared pants and V-neck top. She had already found several pairs of dance shoes for him to choose from. Her favourite was a black pair with white highlighted sides.

They would be the stand-out couple of the night, of that she was sure.

Chapter 22

"You ready to go shopping?" Maddi poked her head into Rory's room.

"You betcha." She raked a gel-covered hand through her hair, spiking it at various angles. She wiped the remainder down the leg of her shorts before grabbing her bag and throwing it over her shoulder. "Let's go!"

They were off on a spending spree. Maddi still had to find an outfit and some new heels for the comps. She hadn't had to buy dance heels before, only flats, so she was quite excited to see what was out there.

Dane had given her a list of the best places to buy Latin performance wear. He had told her to buy whatever she wanted—as long as she could move in it—and he would find something to match.

They decided to find a dress first, and then hopefully they could find some shoes to complement it.

Maddi wasn't really sure what she was looking for, that's why she had Rory with her. She had an eye for fashion and wouldn't let Maddi wear anything unflattering.

"Oh my God! You have to try this on!" Rory held up a white dress with a plunging neckline and no back.

"There's not really much to it, is there?" Maddi said, fingering the fine fabric with a scrunched-up nose.

"Nope. That's kinda the point. It'll look hot!" Rory held it out to her. "At least try it. I bet it looks amazing on." She smiled, rummaging through another rack. "Ooh, this one is gorgeous!" she squealed.

Maddi ended up with an armload of dresses in all different shades. She had to tell Rory to stop pulling any more out or she would collapse from the weight. She found a changing room and hung them on the hangers and over the door. One by one, she tried them on and paraded in front of Rory, twisting and turning to see them from every angle. She even did a few basic steps in front of the mirror to see how the dresses moved on her.

They had narrowed it down to three dresses. One black, one purple, and one emerald green. She tried each one on again, doing some of the shine steps, while watching herself in the mirror.

"I think the black one doesn't have quite enough give in it. It might be quite tricky to do some of the lifts," she said, pressing her lips together.

"Yeah, you're probably right. It's a pity though."

"I know. It's so beautiful." Maddi sighed. "I'm sure there'll be a next time." She went back to the changing room, slipping the black dress off and the purple one on.

Again, she danced in front of the mirror. This one was longer, but the skirt was cut into a V so there were splits up to her hips. She could definitely move more in this one, but the cut of the top just wasn't sitting quite right on her.

The emerald dress had a tight bodice with a halter top, leaving her back bare. The skirt was short, made of hundreds of threads of tassel in the same colour. She had the most freedom in this dress, and it looked fantastic on her.

"This is the one," Maddi said with a smile.

"You do look pretty amazing in it," Rory agreed. "I think some fishnets underneath would finish it off."

"I think you might be right. I'll grab a pair of those ones I saw by the counter." She took one last look in the mirror before changing back into her jeans.

Purchase in hand, they made their way to the shoe shops. Finding shoes to match this colour could be tricky, but there was no way they could have left with any other dress. This one was made for her.

Maddi was surprised at how many different varieties of shoes were available. There was wall upon wall, upon wall. Diamantes and sequins adorning the majority of them. She had never seen so much bling in one place before. She stared in wonder, like a child in a lolly shop for the first time.

And the colours! It was like a rainbow. Every shade imaginable seemed to be on those walls.

"It's breath-taking," Maddi exclaimed with a sigh. "Have you ever seen anything so beautiful?" she asked. Rory was just as dumbfounded as she was.

"It's like a pack of skittles exploded in here." She turned in a circle, staring at the walls. Maddi couldn't help but giggle at the awe on her face.

"You look like you're in heaven."

"Are you kidding me? I want one of every pair!" Rory clapped her hands to her cheeks. "Which ones are you going to choose?"

"I don't even know where to begin."

"Perhaps I can be of some assistance?" An older lady with greying hair pulled back into a severe bun, approached.

"Oh, yes please," Maddi gushed. "I'm entering my first competition and need some heels. I've never had any before."

"Oh, lovely. I used to compete in my younger years. Come this way." She directed them to a wall with what looked to be lower heels. "These are our one-and-a-half inch heels, which are normally what I would recommend for beginners."

"Okay, that's probably me then." Maddi scanned the shelves, eyeing up a black satin pair with emerald diamantes lining the strap.

"Good choice." The lady smiled, pulling them down from the rack. She looked at Maddi's feet. "These should fit. Give them a try."

Maddi sat on one of the stools and slid her feet out of her flats and into the heels held out to her. She had to be shown how to strap them up properly, but once they were on, they looked fantastic.

"Stand up, walk around in them, make sure they are comfortable. You want them to be firm, but not too tight. They will mould to the shape of your foot over time."

"Okay." She stood and took a few cautious steps.

"How do they feel?"

"I can honestly say, these are the most comfortable pair of shoes I have ever worn in my entire life," she said, quickening her pace. She danced down the length of the room. "It's like they're hugging my feet. I love them!" She pointed her toes at Rory.

"What do you think?"

"I'm happy if you are."

"That was easier than I thought it would be," she said, turning to the lady with a grin. "I'll take them please."

She was given a shoe brush to keep the soles in good condition and a bag to store them in.

"Now, make sure you break them in before the competition. You don't want to get blisters during a performance." The lady smiled, patting her hand. "Good luck, dear."

"Thanks for all your help." Maddi smiled back, giving her hand a squeeze.

"Well, now that that's done," Rory said, linking her arm through Maddi's, "how about some lunch? I'm starving!"

Chapter 23

By some miracle, Maddi had managed to avoid Sacha for the past few weeks. They had both been caught up in their own training schedules that their paths hadn't crossed. That was all about to change, however. No matter how much she wanted to, she couldn't hide from her forever, and they had troupe training today—the first one back since their performance at Feeney's.

Maddi was dreading seeing her. After that initial session where she first met Sacha, they had come to an understanding and just left each other alone. Now, with the competition so close, and the confrontation at Feeney's, Maddi was worried what might happen.

She dragged her feet, walking slower than her usual quick pace, trying to put off the inevitable. Pausing outside the entrance, she took several calming breaths, before marching through the door, head held high in false bravado.

She had to force herself to keep her eyes forward as she made a beeline for the seats by the window. Sitting down, she pulled her trusty jazz shoes from her bag and slipped them on. She could feel Sacha's devil stare on her but refused to be drawn into it. She moved to a clear area and began to warm up.

Thankfully, Rachel walked in before Sacha had a chance to approach her.

"Alright guys, let's get to work!" She jogged up to the front of the room. "Have you all warmed up?" Everyone nodded. "Great. I've got a few suggestions for the routine. Take your places." She waited for them to get into position, and they walked through the steps they had memorised, incorporating the new moves and styles into the old.

After going over them a few times, she switched the music on for them to try it at full speed.

"Looking good!" she yelled, bopping her head to the beat as she watched. "Sharpen those arms, ladies!"

The next time she played it through, she joined in with them, taking her place beside Maddi.

"I like the new changes. Brings it all together." She smiled.

"Thanks, I thought so too. I just felt like it was missing something."

They continued dancing for another hour before stopping for a drink break. Maddi grabbed a towel and wiped her neck and face, catching her breath. As much as she had been dreading it, she was glad she had come. Seeing the routine take on a new shape, and perfecting their moves, it was very satisfying.

"Gather round, girls!" Rachel called out. "Firstly, I want to thank you all for your hard work today. I know it can be hard to make changes this far into a routine, but you've all done such a good job of it." She smiled. "I had a lot of great feedback after our performance at Feeney's." She paused, looking each of them in the eye. "I even had people suggest we take it to the comps. What do you think?" she asked.

"Are you kidding? I'm totally in."

"I'm in."

"Me too."

"Sounds good."

"Count me in too. But I am *not* competing with *her*." Sacha glared at Maddi.

"Is that really necessary?" Rachel folded her arms across her chest, disapproval on her face. "We're a team."

"No, *we're* a team." Sacha gestured to the surrounding girls. "We've busted our arses over the last few months to get this routine down, and just like that, she gets to compete with us?" Sacha's hands landed on her hips. "Doesn't seem fair."

"That's uncalled for, Sacha. Maddi is just as much a part of our team as you are. She may not have been with us that long, but she has certainly pulled her weight."

Sacha opened her mouth to speak, but Maddi jumped in first. "It's okay, Rachel. I don't mind," she said, placing her hand on Rachel's arm. "Sacha's right. You guys deserve this. You've worked really hard for it."

"So have you," Rachel said, and the others all agreed.

"Really, it's okay. Gives me more time to focus on my own competition material." She smiled. "You guys are gonna blow them away."

"It won't be the same without you." One of the girls said, giving her a hug.

"Hey, I'll still be there cheering you on." Maddi grinned. "You can't get rid of me that easily."

"If only," Sacha mumbled under her breath. Maddi heard, but chose to ignore her. She couldn't understand why Sacha hated her so much, she was hardly a threat. Sacha had the guy, the moves, the body—what could she possibly be threatened by?

"You know what, Sacha? I had actually hoped we could be adults about all this. Obviously, I was wrong." She sighed. "I don't know what it is you want from me."

"What I want, is for you to disappear. *I* am the Queen of this domain."

"I don't know what you think I'm trying to do, but I have no interest in taking over. I just want to dance," Maddi said simply.

"If that's true, then you won't mind backing out of the comps, will you?" Sacha scowled, hands on hips.

"I'm not going to do that. I made a promise to a friend, and I don't break my promises." She gathered her gear in her arms. "Now, if you'll excuse me, I have somewhere to be." She pushed past Sacha and headed for the door.

Chapter 24

Maddi walked through the door and immediately slumped against the wall. She hated confrontations, they always made her feel flustered. For no real reason, tears filled her eyes.

Pull it together, Maddi. You're better than this.

Placing her hands on her thighs, she took three deep breaths, then made herself start walking. She didn't want Sacha to have the satisfaction of thinking she was rattled.

She retrieved her phone from her back pocket and sent Dane a text to let him know she was finished early. She didn't bother informing him of the 'discussion' her and Sacha had just had. There was no point rocking the boat even more.

They were planning on having a dress rehearsal today, to make sure that there were no costume malfunctions on the big day. After all the hard work they had put in over the past few weeks, she wasn't going to let something so simple and preventable, hinder their performance.

She was actually looking forward to seeing what it looked like all together. As per usual, Rory was going to film them, so they could go over it after. She didn't know what she would do without her.

Neither one of them had seen the other's outfit. Maddi had only shown Dane her shoes, so he had an idea of colour, but that was all. She couldn't wait to see what he was wearing. The anticipation was rather exciting.

With that in mind, she picked up her pace. It would take her a while to get organised with hair and make-up to do as well. For her hair, she would have an intricate plait on each side with glittering sequins to match her dress, plus swirls of colour down the side of her face by her eye, false lashes, and shimmering gloss for her lips - that was the plan anyway. She was putting her faith in Rory to pull it all together.

"Rory! You home?" she called out, bursting through the door.

"In here!" As per usual, Rory was in the kitchen, covered in flour. "I'm making cupcakes." She grinned.

"Perfect. We'll need them for sustenance after rehearsal," Maddi said, swiping her finger through the batter in the bowl and popping it into her mouth.

"There won't be any left if you eat all my batter!" Rory laughed, batting her hands away as she attempted another swipe.

"Fine." Maddi pouted, poking her tongue out. "You still okay to help me today?"

"Of course. I'll just get these in the oven, then I'm all yours." She busied herself scooping batter into cupcake cases, humming to a tune in her head.

Maddi went to her bedroom. She carefully pulled her costume out of her wardrobe and lay it on the bed. She still couldn't believe she got to wear something so beautiful. Even through the plastic covering it, you could see how magnificent it was.

She tore her eyes away and grabbed her dance tights and fishnets to add to the pile. She padded back to the kitchen and through to the bathroom.

"I'm just gonna have a quick shower before I get ready," she said on her way past. "Won't be long."

"I'll be here," Rory said, sliding the tray into the oven and setting the timer. She wiped her hands on her apron before untying it and hanging it on its hook. The cupcakes would take a few minutes to cook, so she ran and gathered her make-up kit, hairspray, and clips, setting them up on the kitchen counter with a mirror.

Maddi came back through, wrapped in a towel.

"Time to get pretty!" she squealed excitedly, almost forgetting that it wasn't the real deal.

While she ran to get changed, Rory pulled the cupcakes from the oven and set them on a wire rack to cool. Adorning her apron once more, she set to work making the buttercream icing to go on top.

She had just set the mixer on auto when there was a knock at the door.

"Can you get that?" Maddi called out.

"Coming!" Rory bellowed as she skipped down the hall to the door. "Hey, come on in. Maddi's just changing."

Dane stepped in, holding up his bag. "Yeah, I still need to do that. Didn't fancy walking over here in a Lycra shirt." He grinned.

"You can use my room if you want." She gestured to the door on her left. "I'll be in the kitchen."

"Thanks."

Rory knocked on Maddi's door as she passed, "Dane's here. He's just getting ready in my room."

"Thanks! I'll be out soon." She sat on her bed, pulling the fishnets carefully over her flesh-coloured dance tights, making sure they weren't twisted. Easing the dress out of its plastic sleeve, she slipped it on and studied her reflection. The brilliant emerald made her ice-blue eyes seem even brighter. Rory had been right about the fishnets too; they really did finish off the outfit.

She opened the door and peeked out. "Okay, here I come." She walked into the lounge. Dane was wearing shiny black dance pants and a Lycra V-neck shirt with emerald sequins to match her dress. "Wow. You look great!" She beamed.

"So do you," Dane managed, eyes glued to her. "You look… beautiful."

Maddi felt her cheeks flush. She ran her hand nervously through her hair. "Thanks."

"Ready for your make-over?" Rory asked.

"Uh-huh," Maddi stammered, uncomfortable under Dane's watchful gaze.

"Sit." Picking up a comb, Rory began raking it through her hair, dividing it into sections. With nimble fingers, she quickly got to work on the plaits, weaving emerald-sequined ribbons through as she went. "Done," she announced, securing the final pin. "Now, head up." She tilted her face up, brush in hand, and painted a sequence of swirls down one side of her face, applying diamantes along the edges.

"That looks great, Rory," Dane said, impressed.

"She certainly has an eye for fashion," Maddi agreed, checking herself out in the hand mirror she was holding.

"She's got a good palette to work on too." Dane grinned cheekily.

"And the award for cheesiest comment goes to…" Rory mocked, doing an imaginary drum roll.

"Yeah, yeah, sorry. Shall we get started?"

"Sure." Maddi placed the mirror on the table behind her and stood up, smoothing the tassels on her dress down. "Let's do it."

Rory took her place in the corner of the room to film, while Dane hooked his iPod up to their speakers.

"Ready?" he asked.

"Ready."

"And… Go!" Rory said, pushing record on her phone. The sound of the guitar solo flooded the room as Dane and Maddi began their routine.

They moved fluidly between their solo shine steps and their partnered combinations, throwing in a few dips and lifts to fit with the hits in the music. Maddi's tassels flicked around her body with every step, accentuating her hip movements. The plunging V-neck of Dane's shirt allowed a view of his perfectly sculpted chest. Altogether, the performance was faultless. No wardrobe malfunctions, no stumbles—pure perfection.

"You two look fantastic!" Rory gushed when the music had come to an end, and they were panting in their final position. "I'm so proud of you!" She clapped her hands together, almost dropping her phone in the process. "Come and look! You're gonna be amazed at how good you look."

Maddi clambered onto the arm of the sofa to get a look at the screen, Dane stood on the other side of Rory.

"Oh wow." Maddi sighed in delight. "I never imagined it would look like that. We really do look amazing." She smiled at Dane.

"I knew we would." He returned her smile with a wink. "Told ya we make a good team."

Chapter 25

For the next week, Maddi dragged herself out of bed every morning for a run before Dane joined her for a training session. They wanted to cram in as much rehearsal as possible before the big day. They had made a few tweaks here and there in their routine, but for the most part, it was competition ready. They knew it inside and out, and even had a few backup moves in place, for any mishaps on the night.

Despite the awkward situation that had prompted their entry into the competition, Maddi was feeling good about it all. She loved having Dane as a dance partner—he challenged her, which she liked. Of course, they had their disagreements, as any partnership does, but they always managed to work past it.

After their final rehearsal before the comps, Maddi sat in her room, wrapped in a towel, staring vacantly at the wardrobe that appeared to have nothing appealing in it. She let out a heavy sigh.

"What's up?" Rory asked as she threw herself across Maddi's bed. "You seem tense." She poked at Maddi's arms and shoulders until she swatted her away.

"I have nothing to wear!" She threw her hands up in disgust. "All of these clothes," she waved her arm about, "and nothing I want to wear. Not. A. Thing. I keep staring at it, hoping something will magically appear."

Rory laughed as she sat up and began massaging Maddi's shoulders. "You wanna raid my wardrobe? I have heaps that would look cute on you."

"I don't know. I guess." Maddi slumped down. "What's wrong with me? I feel so… emotional." She sighed, looking down at her fingers twisting in her lap.

"It's just nerves. You've been working your arse off for the last few months, and now it's almost at an end. It's natural to be emotional." She gave her shoulders a squeeze. "But you have nothing to worry about. You're gonna be great."

Maddi attempted a smile. "Thanks."

"Come on." Rory gave her a gentle push. "Get up, let's go see what we can find in my wardrobe for you to wear."

"Okay." Maddi reluctantly stood, allowing herself to be led across the hall. Rory sat her down on her bed and began pulling all manner of garments from her hangers and drawers. Within seconds, she had a large pile for Maddi to sift through and find something to her liking.

"You look through here, and I'll go whip us up a coffee and some cake."

"Cake for breakfast?" Maddi questioned.

"Damn straight! Breakfast of champions." Rory winked before bounding out the door to the kitchen.

Maddi knelt on the floor and began picking through the pile of clothes scattered around her. She chose a lilac, off-the-shoulder sweater with a pair of three-quarter length jeans covered in colourful patches. She ran her fingers through her hair and pulled it up into a ponytail before padding out to join Rory.

The coffee was ready and waiting, along with a healthy slice of red velvet cake. She had to admit, cake did sound like a pretty great breakfast right now. Perhaps the sugary sweetness would boost her mood.

She scooped up her plate and coffee and made herself comfortable on the couch, curling her feet beneath her.

"Have I told you how much I love you?" she asked Rory, with a mouth full of cake.

"Not today." Rory grinned, wiping the frosting from the sides of her mouth. "Is it working? You feel better?"

"Mmhmm," Maddi mumbled. "Thanks."

"Anytime."

They ate in silence, barely taking a breath between mouthfuls. Maddi's shoulders loosened as the tension from earlier slipped away with every bite. Rory certainly knew how to put her at ease. It was like her superpower.

"So, what's on the agenda for today?" Rory asked after licking the crumbs from her plate.

"Something that doesn't require much thought," Maddi said. "My brain is out of order today."

"Shopping it is!" Rory announced. "You can help me find something to wear for tomorrow night."

"Ooh sounds fun!" Maddi perked up. "What kind of look are we going for?"

"Hmm," Rory considered. "Chic meets street."

"Whatever that means." Maddi laughed. "Come on then, let's get going. This could take all day." They each placed their plates in the sink, ready to wash, before running to their rooms to grab the essentials—shoes, purse, and lip gloss. Pulling the door closed behind them, they linked arms and walked down the path towards the mall.

Several hours, and shops later, the girls emerged from the brightly lit mall, blinking their eyes as they adjusted to the natural light of the day. Not only had they managed to find Rory the perfect mix of 'chic meets street', but also a pair of grungy, lace-up boots to match, a funky beret-style cap, and some hair dye to finish it off. Rory's already short peroxide blonde hair was about to have some purple streaks put through it, care of Maddi.

Rory had a style all of her own and was forever changing her hair. In the years they had known each other, she had had all manner of cuts—long with layers, braids, bobs—you name it, she'd had it. Boredom played a large part in that, as did keeping up with the latest trends. This pixie cut, however, had managed to stay the course the longest, the only change being to the colour. She was able to style it in various ways with gel, keeping the boredom at bay.

Maddi couldn't wait to see what the streaks would look like. They had chosen a deep purple colour, hoping it would lighten up once added to the peroxide already present in her hair. She was to put streaks through the bulk of it, with thick foils in the front.

It would be her first attempt at streaking someone's hair—hence the beret—just in case it didn't quite go to plan. Whatever happened, Rory was going to look fantastic. They'd covered all the bases.

Chapter 26

The following morning, Maddi was up and in the kitchen, preparing breakfast at an unspeakable hour. Nerves had gotten the better of her during the night and she had tossed and turned for hours.

Retrieving the pancake batter from the fridge where it had been chilling for the past hour, she gave it one last whisk. She placed a blob of butter into a hot frying pan and began to spoon the mixture in, swirling it to spread it out.

While she waited for the first side to cook, she flicked the jug on and pulled two cups down from the shelf. She knew it wouldn't be long before Rory stumbled out upon smelling the goings on in the kitchen. She was surprised the bacon crisping in the oven hadn't already drawn her out.

Considering her lack of sleep, she was feeling surprisingly chipper this morning. Prancing about the kitchen in her pink bunny slippers and robe, she allowed herself to feel excited about the evening ahead. They had worked so hard over the past few months; it would be great to finally show everyone what they were capable of. And by everyone, she meant Sacha.

She flipped the first pancake over, then pulled the bacon from the oven. She brought out two plates and the maple syrup. Once the jug had switched itself off, she poured their coffees and called out to Rory.

"I made you breakfast." She grinned, holding the plate out to her dishevelled flatmate. Rory's purple and blonde hair stuck out at all angles, like some sort of new era hedgehog. As if on cue, she ran her fingers through it, softening the spikes, while she yawned and staggered to the kitchen.

"Mmm, I thought I could smell bacon," she said, reaching for the plate. She poured an extra helping of syrup over her already drenched pancakes.

"Coffee's over there." Maddi pointed at the bench with one hand, while pouring the next lot of batter into the pan.

"You're up early."

"Couldn't sleep. Stupid nerves," she grumbled light-heartedly. "At least I get to enjoy the sunshine though." She smiled, looking out the kitchen window.

"Aren't nerves meant to be a good thing? Adrenalin and all that?"

"Provided I don't crash and burn before our performance."

"You'll be too wired for that to happen. Red Bull, my friend. That'll get you through." Rory shovelled a forkful of dripping pancake and bacon into her mouth. "Mmm, this is good." A trickle of syrup made its way down her chin, and she tried to lick it up with her tongue.

"I hope so, I'm starving." Maddi flipped her pancake onto her plate and piled several pieces of bacon on top, followed by the maple syrup. "I've been waiting all morning for this." She eyed her plate hungrily before scooping some into her mouth. "Oh yeah," she mumbled with her mouth full.

"Mmhmm," Rory agreed. She was licking the plate clean, making sure she got every last drop.

"I think you got it," Maddi laughed, almost choking on her food. One of the things she loved most about Rory was her childlike behaviour. How she couldn't care less what people thought of her, or her actions. In return, Maddi could also act the fool and Rory wouldn't even bat an eye. In fact, she was likely to join in.

"What time do you have to be there today?"

"The competitors have to meet at lunch to walk through stage settings. That should take an hour or so, and then it's time to get ready," Maddi said with a smile.

"So, I'll meet you there around two to get your hair and makeup done?"

"Yeah. Thanks, Rory. I don't know what I'd do without you."

"Anytime, babe. That's what I'm here for."

Down at the venue, Dane was pacing back and forth waiting for Maddi to arrive. He kept patting his pocket to check he had their music, even though he had a backup in his bag. A dream the night before had made him paranoid that they would have the wrong music playing and it would ruin their routine. The first thing he did when he got up, was to check it and make a copy so there could be no mistakes.

The door opened, and in breezed Sacha and Jessie. They looked just as nervous as he felt. Jessie saw him watching and offered a small wave. Dane simply nodded in their direction.

Maddi came bounding up behind him. "Hey."

"Hey, yourself." Dane grinned as he turned to face her. "How you feeling?"

"A little tired, but other than that, pretty good."

"Couldn't sleep either, huh?" Dane had spent the night counting the dimples on his ceiling.

"Not really, no. But don't worry, I can still do this." She grinned, her eyes wide as she took in the crowd. "Are all these people competing?"

"Yup. Some will be in teams though. They're not all our competition."

"Oh, of course." She waved at Rachel and the other girls when she spotted them. "This is quite exciting," she gushed. "I've never been to anything like this before."

"Yeah, it is pretty cool," Dane agreed.

"Alright, people! Gather round so I don't have to yell!" A man was standing centre stage holding a clip board. "We have a lot to get through, so if we can stick to the schedule, this will all run smoothly. In a moment, we are going to have all the teams come to the stage in their order of performances so we can get positioning and lighting right. After them, we will have the Beginners Couples, the Intermediate Couples and the Advanced Couples. The schedule is up on the wall." He pointed. "Let's get started!"

One by one, the teams made their way to the stage, taking up their starting positions. Maddi and Dane sat watching.

"Have you seen Sacha and Jessie?" she whispered.

"Yeah, they're back there." He pointed behind him. "I was thinking of going over there."

Maddi pursed her lips. "Is that wise? We don't need to start a fight before the comps, Dane. Let's just keep our distance."

"I was actually thinking of wishing them luck."

"Oh, really?" Her jaw dropped and she scooted back in her seat. "You've had a change of heart."

"Yeah. I guess. You do a lot of thinking when you can't sleep." He chuckled, scrubbing a hand across his chin. "I just don't want to be angry anymore."

"Good for you." She smiled encouragingly. "Do you want me to go with you?"

"If you want." He shrugged his shoulders but offered his hand as he stood up. Together they walked over to where the others were seated.

"Sacha. Jessie." Dane nodded at each of them. "I just… *We* just wanted to wish you luck tonight." He offered his hand.

"Thanks, man," Jessie said, standing to shake hands. "That means a lot."

"We're not the ones who need luck," Sacha smirked.

"Sacha!" Jessie looked at her with an embarrassed look.

"What? Don't think that coming over here and acting all nice as pie is going to change the fact that we have a bet on."

"I wasn't trying to get out of anything. I just wanted to put this shit behind us."

"Fine by me, but a bet's a bet. If we win, you still have to find another dance partner," she sneered.

"Just because I wish you good luck, doesn't mean we're giving up. We're still in this to win it." He folded his arms across his chest.

"Bring it on." Sacha held her arms out in challenge.

Maddi stepped between Dane and Sacha, looking her up and down. "Oh, we will, don't you worry."

Chapter 27

"Ladies and Gentlemen! Welcome to the annual National Salsa Championships!" There was a loud cheer from the audience. "We have a fantastic show lined up for you tonight! These dancers have put everything they have into making this a show to remember, so sit back and enjoy! First up tonight, we have the teams!"

Backstage, there were bodies running around everywhere. Two teams were lined up, ready to get on stage, while the others were busy putting on the finishing touches to their make-up or having last minute run-throughs.

Rory was applying the diamantes to Maddi's face while she touched up her lipstick.

"I'm so nervous!" she blurted, waving her hands in front of her. "I can't sit still."

"Nearly done," Rory said, her fingers pressing the last one down. "There." She held Maddi's chin between her finger and thumb, admiring her handy work. "Not bad, even if I do say so myself."

Maddi stood, checking herself out in the full-length mirror provided. Her hair glistened with the glitter hairspray Rory had used, the sequins catching the light every time she moved. It was going to look great on stage.

"I'd better head out. Don't want to miss your performance!" Rory grinned, giving Maddi a big hug. "Break a leg!" She squeezed her tight, before planting a kiss on her cheek. She fought her way through the throngs of competitors and out the door.

The first team came barging back through the changing room, giggling and chattering excitedly.

"Oh my God! That was so much fun!"

"I know! I was so sure I was going to fall."

"I missed the turn!"

"You were great, no-one would've even noticed."

Maddi smiled as she listened to their enthusiastic banter. She scanned the list on the wall to see when Rachel and the girls would be making their way to the stage—they were the last team in their category. Maddi rushed out to find them, wanting to wish them luck before they went on.

"Rachel!" she called out, raising her hand to wave.

"Maddi, hi!" Rachel said. "Can you believe this? Who knew there were so many amazing dancers in New Zealand?" She grinned.

"I just wanted to wish you and the girls the best of luck. You're gonna be fabulous!" She beamed, pulling them in for a group hug.

The next team came running down the stairs, and their name was called out.

"This is it!" Rachel turned to the front, leading her team to the stage. Maddi cheered them on from the side-lines. They looked fantastic in their tiny black shorts, tight white tees and black suspenders. Their hair was pulled back in tight buns, with black top-hats adorning their heads.

The audience clapped and whooped as they made their way off the stage with huge grins on their faces. Sacha pushed her way to the front, shoving Maddi aside.

"Out of my way! I have to get changed."

"Rude," Maddi muttered under her breath. She brushed her hands down her dress, making sure everything was in place then went to find Dane out back.

"Where have you been?" he demanded when he spotted her.

"Sorry, I was watching the girls perform. Did you want me for something?" she asked.

"Sorry, I just freaked out. I thought you had backed out,' he admitted sheepishly.

"Dane, we're in this together. I wouldn't just leave." She touched his arm gently.

"I know. I guess I'm just a little paranoid." He ran his hand through his hair restlessly. "You look great, by the way," he added with a smile.

"Thanks, so do you." She smiled warmly. "You ready for this? We're up soon."

"Yeah, I'm ready." He let out the breath he had been holding, shaking his head side-to-side like a boxer preparing for a fight.

The beginner couples started to line up by the stage door. Some looked as though they may throw up, others chattered nervously. There were only three couples in this category, and Maddi was impressed at their courage. To be in the beginner category, both dancers had to have been dancing for a maximum of six months and had no performance experience.

Because Dane had been dancing longer and they had both performed before, they were put in the intermediate section. It was the same for Sacha and Jessie. There were four couples in their category, one on either side of them. Maddi and Dane would be performing third in line.

One by one, the beginners made their way up the stairs to the stage, each time reappearing with a look of relief. Performing in front of a crowd took a bit of getting used to, but there was nothing quite like the rush of being on stage, under the lights, and hearing people applaud for you.

"Intermediate couples to the stage door please," the man with the clipboard said as he rushed down the hall.

Maddi's face lit up with anticipation. She gripped Dane's arm and jumped up and down on the spot. Her enthusiasm was infectious, and soon he was grinning along with her.

"Come on then, let's go line up," he said with a laugh.

They stood behind Sacha and Jessie. She feigned indifference, while Jessie smiled nervously at them.

"Good luck," he whispered after the first couple took to the stage.

"You too," Maddi said back. She grabbed Dane's hand and gave it a squeeze. "I still can't believe we're really here!" she said excitedly.

"Well, believe it. It won't be the last time, I can guarantee it." He smiled down at her, patting her hand.

The doors swung open and they heard the announcer's voice. "What a lovely couple! Let's give them another round of applause!" The stage director motioned for Sacha and Jessie to move up to the curtains, ready for their entrance.

"Our next couple to the stage are a new partnership, let's see what they've got for us! Put your hands together for Sacha Barret and Jessie Jameson!"

Sacha plastered a smile across her face and strutted out onto the stage. They took up their positions, waiting for the music.

Maddi and Dane crept up to the curtains to watch, they wanted to see what they were up against.

The music blared, and Maddi could feel Dane grow tense. He was flexing his hand by his side, as if ready to throw a punch, and the look on his face was pure murder. She had no idea what had caused this sudden change in his mood, but it obviously had something to do with Sacha. The longer he watched them, the deeper the scowl on his face became.

Maddi bit her lip, her eyes darting back and forth between the stage and Dane. The song was almost over and then it would be their turn. She needed him to focus, or they would lose the bet.

Doing the only thing she could think of, she grabbed his hand and dragged him away from the stage.

She reached her hands up to cup his face and pulled him towards her, planting a soft kiss on his lips.

His eyes grew wide at the shock, but then he began to kiss her back with an eagerness. He crushed his lips against hers, pulling her body in close as he ran his fingers down her back.

The music came to an end and the room erupted into applause. Maddi pulled away, giving Dane a small smile.

"What was that about?" he asked with a goofy grin on his face.

"Just because," Maddi said quietly. "Come on, we're up." She took his hand and intentionally led him to the back of the stage, away from where Sacha would be leaving from.

"Let's welcome our next couple to the stage! Give a warm welcome to Maddison Lee and Dane Rogers!"

"Let's do this!" Maddi winked. Dane offered his elbow, and they made their way to the centre of the stage. He spun her a few times, letting her go to get to her position. They stood opposite each other, hands on their hips and faces dipped down. The audience was silent as they waited with anticipation.

"Go, Maddi!" Rory called from the crowd, doing her best wolf whistle. Maddi's smile stretched even wider as she listened to her friend make all kinds of noises in the silence.

The beautiful sound of a guitar rang through the speakers, and both Maddi and Dane came to life. Out of the corner of her eye, she could see Dane was giving it everything he had. She had never seen him dance with such passion before. He flashed a smile in her direction as they turned to face each other, ready for the next part of their routine.

It all happened so fast. One minute they were dancing, and the next, they were doing their final lift, puffing and panting, listening to the cheers of the crowd. Of course, Rory was the loudest of them all.

"Woohoo!" she hollered through cupped hands. "That's my best friend!" she yelled enthusiastically to anyone who would listen.

Dane lowered Maddi to the ground, and they walked to the front of the stage for their bow. Maddi could see Rory jumping up and down, waving. She couldn't help but giggle at the sight.

Turning, they both marched off the stage and down the stairs.

"Oh, man, that was amazing! You were on fire!" Maddi could barely contain herself. She was giddy with adrenalin.

"You were pretty amazing yourself." Dane grinned, happy to see her like this. "That kiss kinda spurred me on," he admitted.

"Yeah? I'm glad," Maddi said, suddenly feeling shy. "It just felt like the right time."

"It was the perfect time. I'm glad you did it." He reached for her hand. "You're welcome to do it any time you like." Maddi smiled, feeling her face flush. "Maybe we could go on a date sometime?" he asked, his voice full of hope.

"Yeah, I think I'd like that," Maddi said, genuinely surprised at herself. She hadn't really thought it through before, it had been a spur of the moment thing, but she couldn't see the harm in seeing where it went. Dane was a nice enough guy, and they *did* make a good team.

Chapter 28

"You!" Dane's face clouded over, and he was filled with rage once more. Maddi turned to see who he was talking to—Sacha—of course, she should have known. No one else could have that effect on him.

"Me?" Sacha pointed at herself, looking side-to-side.

"Yes, you! Who else?" Dane spat as he stormed towards her. Sacha took a step back, a look of panic on her face. She held her hands up as if to fend him off, but Jessie stepped in front of her.

"Is everything okay, Dane?" he asked, placing a hand on his chest, "you seem upset."

"That's an understatement!" He shoved Jessie against the wall. "Her I expected this from, but not you! To think, I actually thought you were sorry for what you did to me."

"Woah, man! I have no idea what you're talking about!" Jessie held his arms up, palms out. He frowned.

"The hell you don't!" Dane barked.

Maddi put her hand on his arm. "Dane?" she questioned, just as confused as Jessie. "Why don't we calm down and talk about this?" She pulled his arm away from Jessie's chest, turning him to look at her.

His eyes softened, and he dropped his hands to his sides. Taking a deep breath, he managed to calm himself down enough to speak without drawing so much attention to them.

"They stole my routine," he said to Maddi.

"They *what*?" She looked at Jessie incredulously.

"Now, hang on…" he started but Dane shut him down with a look.

"I choreographed that routine for me and Sacha. They used my work against me."

"Sacha?" Jessie turned to look at her. The smug look on her face told him Dane was telling the truth. "You did that?" he asked, mouth gaping open in shock.

"Don't act so surprised. What else was I going to do? There wasn't time to start from scratch, and it's not like he was going to use it." Sacha took a defensive stance.

"I can't believe you did that," Jessie said quietly. He turned to Dane. "I'm so sorry. I honestly had no idea."

Dane huffed, clearly unimpressed by the apology. "You know what? I'm glad you two found each other. Now I can see you for who you really are, Sacha. You're only out for number one." He swung his gaze to Jessie. "You better watch your back. Once a cheater, always a cheater." He draped his arm around Maddi's shoulders. "Come on, they'll be announcing the winners soon."

They walked away, leaving Jessie to deal with Sacha. Maddi almost felt sorry for him. Almost.

"Alright, ladies and gentlemen! Now for the moment you've all been waiting for! The results!" the host announced as he was handed a card from the judges.

There was a hush over the audience as the competitors filed back on stage, gathered in a large group, arms around each other.

Sacha was standing with her teammates, while Jessie stood to the back of the group. He had his hands in his pockets and was looking at the floor.

Dane wrapped his arm firmly around Maddi's waist, pulling her in close and kissing the top of her head. She scanned the audience in front of her, watching as Rory bopped up and down like a yo-yo. She wondered what the person behind her thought of all that.

Each of the teams who had placed were standing at the front of the stage, holding their medals and certificates up for all to see. Someone jumped out with a camera, snapping pics of the winners.

Maddi applauded with the audience, cheering loudest for Rachel's team who had taken out first place. They all shuffled along, so that the beginners were closest to the host. Maddi reached out and squeezed Rachel's arm as she passed her by. She winked and gave her a thumbs up.

The butterflies in her stomach were throwing a party. She was more nervous now, than she had been before performing. More than just reputations were on the line. If they didn't beat Sacha and Jessie, she and Dane would have to find new dance partners. On the other hand, if they won, she wouldn't have to see Sacha anymore.

She crossed her fingers behind her back and said a silent prayer.

"Now for the Intermediate couples! We had some fierce competition this year! The votes are in, and it was a close one!" the host bellowed through the microphone. "Coming in third place is… Nadine and Rob!" They stepped forward and accepted their awards. "With only three points between them and first place, the second place goes to… Sacha and Jessie!"

Jessie's head snapped up when he heard his name. Sacha latched onto his elbow as they made their way to the front. She gave Maddi a smug smile over her shoulder.

"And the winner of the Intermediate couples' section is… Dane and Maddi!" The audience erupted in a bout of cheers and whoops, led by Rory.

Dane pulled Maddi into his arms, lifting her off her feet and planting a kiss on her lips. "We did it!" he cried. Maddi giggled, flinging her arms around his neck. They collected their medals, and someone handed Maddi a bouquet of flowers.

Joining their fellow winners for photos, Maddi snuck a peek at Sacha. The smugness had been wiped from her face and replaced with a bitter smile as she tried to pretend it didn't matter.

When it was all over, and they were no longer in front of an audience, Dane walked up to Sacha and Jessie, towing Maddi behind him.

"Nice work," he said, "I guess we'll see you around sometime. Oh, that's right. No, we won't," he smiled from ear-to-ear. "I seem to recall that we had a bet. You'll have to find another bar to frequent. Sorry." He turned on his heels, stifling the laughter bubbling up inside.

Maddi giggled, "That was mean," she whispered.

"Admit it, you enjoyed it too."

"Maybe just a little." She held her finger and thumb together, leaving the tiniest of gaps. Dane threw his arm around her shoulder again, and together, they walked out to meet Rory.

Chapter 29

"Hurry up! He'll be here soon," Maddi said impatiently as Rory weaved her fingers through her hair.

"Shut up and sit still. I swear you're worse than a three-year old!" She had bobby pins hanging from her mouth, and a look of sheer determination. "Just this little bit here… there! All done," she said proudly.

After the plaits she had perfected for the comps, Rory had become somewhat obsessed with finding new ways to braid hair, and not having a lot of her own, Maddi was her guinea pig, whether she liked it or not.

This particular braid was made up of several small plaits, woven together in a spiral around her head. It was time consuming, but the result was worth it.

"Nice work," Maddi praised. "Will it hold?"

"There's like, a hundred pins in there and half a bottle of hairspray. That baby ain't going anywhere." Rory grinned, spinning the bottle around in her hand cockily.

Maddi stretched her arms above her, twisting her head side-to-side to relieve the cramps from holding it still for so long. She stood, brushing her hands down her front. "Do I look okay?" she asked.

"You look fine. Stop worrying so much!"

"I know I shouldn't be nervous, but I can't help it. First date jitters and all."

There was a knock on the door, making her jump.

"Eee! He's here," she said in an excited whisper.

"Well? What are you waiting for? Go get 'em!" Rory shoved her towards the door. "Have fun!" she called.

Maddi opened the door, grinning goofily. "Hey," she sang with a little wave.

Dane chuckled. "Hey, yourself," he said. "You ready?"

"Yup." She went to walk through the door, misjudging the step down. She stumbled and fell against Dane's chest, his arms circling to catch her.

"Well, I didn't think you'd be throwing yourself at me so soon," he joked, helping her to her feet.

"Ss-sorry about that," she stammered, her cheeks blushing to a rosy colour. "I'm such a klutz."

"I don't know, I think you're a real catch," he grinned, nudging her with his elbow.

Maddi burst out laughing. "That was cheesy!"

"Got you smiling though, didn't it?" He offered her his arm. "Shall we?"

"We shall," she said, looping her arm through his.

"I told you we make a good team."

Follow Maddi, Dane and Sacha in the
sequel "Dancing in Circles"

A note from the Author

Hello! Thank you for taking the time to read my novella "Dancing through the Storm". I hope you enjoyed reading it as much as I enjoyed writing it.

If you happened to enjoy my story, perhaps you could leave a brief review—reviews help authors' work to be seen, as well as providing us with feedback to improve.

Thanks again!

Stacey Broadbent

Other Books by Stacey Broadbent

Standalone

Never Judge a Book
Deep Heat

A Step in Time Series

Dancing Through the Storm
Dancing in Circles
Dancing with Destiny
A Step in Time: the complete series

Hollywood Novels

Emma

Flesh-Eater Series

Fear the Fever
Fight the Fever

Dark Sins Novellas

Sins of the Flesh
Mine

Ink-Slinging Sisters

Awesome Applesauce

Super Mum Series

Frazzled
Frazzled and Frumpy
Frazzled, Frumpy and Fabulous!
Super Mum: the complete series

Short stories and poetry

Musings, Mournings, and Misadventures

Anthologies

The White Ribbon Collection
Scars to your Beautiful
Witching Hour: Vices and Virtues
Key to my Heart
A Touch of Inspiration
No Place like Home
Serendipity

Stacey Broadbent

Acknowledgements

A huge thank you to Launa for being my cheerleader and encouraging me to re-release this series for all to see.

To Trina, my proofreading partner in crime, and number one supporter from the very first words I penned. You mean the world to me.

To all the bloggers who help to promote for all the indie authors out there, you guys rock! I appreciate every share, every review, every mention. You are amazing!

To everyone who has read any of my books, thank you! Without you, I wouldn't be able to do what I love. You make my dream a reality.

Connect with me

http://www.staceybroadbent.weebly.com

https://www.facebook.com/StaceyBroadbentAuthor

Broadbent's Bookish Babes: https://goo.gl/FY9wQN

https://www.amazon.com/author/staceybroadbent

Goodreads: https://goo.gl/YJ6dXa

https://www.instagram.com/authorstaceybroadbent/

https://www.bookbub.com/authors/stacey-broadbent

https://vm.tiktok.com/ZSJBb5bhL/

Sign up for my newsletter:
http://eepurl.com/cULu_f

About the Author

Stacey resides in Ashburton, New Zealand with her husband and three children. She is a qualified proofreader, author, wife, mother, and self-proclaimed culinary goddess. When she's not busy writing or editing books, she enjoys reading and procrastinating on TikTok.

She absolutely loves hearing from readers, so please feel free to reach out via email, Instagram, or join her reader group, Broadbent's Bookish Babes. You can also sign up to her newsletter for up-to-date info on releases.